Forget Me Now

a novel by Alana Terry

CHAPTER 1

Springtime. I've always loved the spring. And today's going to be perfect. It's the senior trip today. Time to get myself up and out of bed.

Ow.

Wait. Why does my head hurt this much?

A knock on my door. Mom? No, she doesn't knock that way. Who is it then?

The door cracks open. "Dad?" I squint at him. Maybe it's because I don't have my contacts in yet. Is that what's wrong? He looks different.

"Dad?" I say the word again because I'm not sure it came out right last time.

"Hiya, Mimi." He's smiling at me. That cheesy grin. I try to remember the last time he came to my room in the morning. Why isn't he at work already?

"Hi," I answer tentatively. My head is swirling with questions, but it's also swirling with pain. Pain and fog and

1

confusion. I think I'm scared, but it's hard to remember.

Remember ...

Dad sits on the corner of my bed. He looks smaller. Maybe it's because he hasn't done this since I was a little girl, coming into my room like this. There's something in his eyes. Like he's embarrassed to tell me something. No, not embarrassed. That's not quite right. So what is it?

Oh, no. Has something happened to Chris? Is that what he came in here to tell me? What if Mr. Gomez finally got arrested? Or even worse, what if his dad beat him up? I know I promised Chris I wouldn't tell about his family, but I didn't know what to do. I had to let somebody know. Did Chris's dad find out and get so mad at him that he ...

"How you feeling?" Dad asks me, and I honestly have no idea how to answer.

He takes a deep breath, and I prepare myself. It's Chris. I know it is. I promised when we started dating that I wouldn't tell anybody about his dad. What could I do? He was crying on my shoulder, just like a terrified little child. And he was blubbering, begging me not to share his secret. So I assured him I wouldn't. I made him a promise.

And now something terrible has happened.

I should never have told ...

But why does my head hurt so much?

Dad clears his throat. "So, baby, do you know what today is?"

What kind of a question is that? Of course I know what today is. It's the last Friday in May. It's senior skip day. Chris and I were planning to …

I glance at the clock. The time is right. Same time Mom wakes me up every morning. That part hasn't changed, except it's Dad here and not Mom. But there's something else not quite right.

Dad's got his hand on top of my blanket, holding down my leg. Does he think I'm about to jump up and sprint out the door? Mom couldn't be having second thoughts about senior skip day, could she? She's been as excited about our camping trip as I have …

So it is Chris. I knew it. Something happened. Something terrible. I shiver a little. Dread? Uncertainty?

"Mia." As soon as Dad says the word, my stomach drops. *Mia.* Not Princess or Mimi or any of those other pet names that he always uses.

Mia.

I try to sit up, but I'm so dizzy. He takes his other hand to keep me down on the bed. Something's glistening in the corner of his eye. I refuse to admit it might be a tear. When's the last time I saw Dad cry? Come to think of it, have I ever seen Dad cry? It must be something else. The bright light shining in from the window, blinding him, making him squint.

Except there's no bright light shining in from the window. Just that early morning gray.

My brain feels like it's trying to tell me something. Trying to wake up or recover some missing piece. But I have no idea what I've forgotten. No idea why Dad's looking at me with a tear in the corner of his eye. No idea why he's the one waking me up instead of Mom.

"Mia, I want you to listen to me very carefully," he says. I stare into his eyes, looking for comfort or strength. Instead, that tear. That one single sparkling tear.

It must be worse than I thought. What if Chris is dead? What if his dad …

"You've been out of it for a little while," Dad says. I want to laugh. You have no idea how much I want to laugh. It's the kind of thing Mom might do. A joke. Like the time she changed my clock then ran into my room and told me I missed my AP psychology test when instead she just wanted to wake me up early so we could go get donuts before she dropped me off at school.

But Dad never jokes. Not like this. And he never gives

surprises.

"What do you mean?" I croak.

Dad sighs, and there's something vaguely familiar about that sigh, like I've heard it before. It's like studying for a calculus exam only to walk into the wrong classroom where the teacher hands you a test in French. The problem is you don't know French because you've been studying Spanish since sixth grade so you can become a doctor and set up a free health clinic along the Mexican border.

In other words, I have no idea what Dad's saying.

"There was an accident," he begins, wincing when he gets out the word. "A terrible accident."

There's something in the way he says it. Something in his voice, his expression. I'm not entirely convinced this is all about Chris anymore. Because if my boyfriend got into an accident and died, Mom would be the one to tell me, and she'd be crying for real, not just sitting here with one single tear in the corner of her eye. Mom adores Chris. Dad not so much. So if there was some kind of accident, if something happened to my boyfriend, Dad wouldn't be the one to come in here and tell me about it. Which can only mean …

I sit up in bed, ignoring the pain in the back of my skull, shaking off the dizziness as best I can. "Where's Mom?" I demand.

Dad's holding my shoulders, trying to pin me down. I think I'm crying, but I'm not sure. My throat feels sore, like it wants to let out a sob. "Where's Mom?" I repeat. "I want to talk to Mom."

And a strange flash, a sort of *deja-vu* flits through my head, but only for a fraction of a second. A fraction of a second that throws me totally off balance, makes me stop struggling so hard. Because I've got this sense I've done this before.

Dad opens his mouth.

"Mom can't be here right now, Mimi. We have to have a talk."

CHAPTER 2

Dad hands me a cup of coffee in one of his masculine travel mugs. Coffee in bed? Is this my dad or has he been taken over by space aliens?

I glance around for my phone on my nightstand. It's reflex, really. Wake up. Sit up in bed. Check for text messages. Because I'm certain that sometime between now and last night when Chris and I got off the phone, my boyfriend texted me. He always does.

"Don't worry about your cell right now," Dad says. Apparently he's become a mind reader all of a sudden. "Drink your coffee," he tells me, and his voice sounds more like him. Controlled. In charge.

I obey but wince. Dad always makes my coffee too sweet. Probably because he's so used to drinking his black. Except I only drink coffee on special occasions, and he's never once brought me a drink in bed.

"Too much sugar?" he asks, glancing slightly away.

"It's perfect." I give him a smile. At least I try to, but it makes my head hurt even more, and now Dad's the one to wince.

"Had enough?" he asks. He takes the mug and places it on my end table, picking up a hot-pink zebra print binder I've never seen before. "Do you know what this is?"

I shake my head. It looks like something I would have begged Mom for when I was back in second grade. The folder is so over-the-top frilly I'm surprised it doesn't have unicorns and glitter.

Dad opens up to the first page and shows me a photograph taped to the inside cover. "Do you know who this is?"

I roll my eyes. At least I start to, but a splintering headache makes me stop.

"That's Chris," I tell him. What in the world is going on?

Dad nods then turns the page.

"And this?"

"It's last Christmas," I answer mechanically. "Mom wanted us to finally get a picture with all four of us in it, except she couldn't figure out how to use that selfie stick you got her." It's a funny memory... except I'm not laughing.

Neither is my dad.

He points to another photo. "Do you know her?"

I blink at the girl with bouncy brown curls. Then blink again. Dad's pointer finger is covering the bottom corner of the picture. I reach out for my glasses, the pair I keep on the end table, but they only make my headache worse.

"Do you know her?" he asks again.

And again I blink. "Kelsie?" I hear the uncertainty in my own voice. It isn't because I've forgotten my best friend. Kelsie and I have been inseparable since middle school. We do everything together, but that still doesn't explain this picture. Still doesn't explain why I'm lying in a strange bed wearing a flowery hospital gown, taking a selfie with Kelsie.

A selfie I don't remember.

What's going on?

Dad leans in a little closer. "Do you know when this picture was taken?"

"No," I whisper. For a minute I wonder if this is some strange photoshop joke. But then I remember that my dad never jokes. Never does anything unexpected.

If this were Mom, she'd be busting a gut laughing by now. Telling me how she paid some graphic design student a few bucks to interpose me and Kelsie into someone else's hospital photo just to see how confused I'd get. Then she'd tell me breakfast was ready, and she'd laugh about it some more while we ate.

But this isn't Mom. This is Dad, and Dad never laughs. He lets out a cough and turns the page. "Do you recognize any of the other people in this picture?" He's leaning closer to me now. So intent. I feel like I did a few weeks ago when he watched me open my acceptance letter to NYU, his alma mater. I was nervous, not because I have my heart set on going to NYU, but because I knew how disappointed Dad would be if I didn't get that scholarship I applied for.

"It's my friends from school," I answer. And there we are. Me and Kelsie. About a dozen others, some holding balloons, get-well posters, all of us posing for the camera. We're in the same hospital room. I'm wearing that same ugly gown, trying to smile.

"Do you remember taking this picture?"

There's an answer Dad's expecting from me, except I can't give it to him. I shake my head.

"No," I tell him, realizing without understanding why that I'm letting him down. But I can't lie. Not about something like this. My heart is racing faster than normal. Just how strong was that coffee?

"Are you sure?" There's a squeeze in Dad's voice, a tension. Which again makes me wonder what all this means or how it is that my answer is hurting him so deeply.

I stare again at the picture. I know these faces. Happy, smiling teens. My friends for years.

But why are we in a hospital room? And why am I dressed in that hideous gown?

Something isn't right. The lump in my throat, the racing of my pulse, they're all telling me the same thing. It's like this is the most important test I've ever taken, and I'm failing miserably. But I can't make up the answers. I shake my head again, look at my dad through these tears I'm trying to blink away, and tell him honestly, "I don't know when that picture was taken. I don't remember a thing."

CHAPTER 3

"It's okay, Mimi. It's okay." Dad is running his hand over my hair, and I can't remember the last time we've had any sort of physical contact like this. Usually it's a half-second hug before bed. If he's even home by the time I turn in for the night. I used to like to kiss the scratch of his cheek, but that was when I was younger. I can't remember the last time I kissed him.

Can't remember ...

"What was I doing in the hospital?" I'm trying not to get hysterical, but I feel the panic welling up inside me. It's like I've lost something but can't even remember what it was so I can properly mourn.

"You had an accident, baby." I hear the strain in his voice, the tension, and yet the words come out so rehearsed. Have I heard them before? "You lost some of your memory."

I'm crying. Sniffling. Trying hard not to sob. Wiping snot on the sleeves of my pajamas. I don't understand. *This isn't funny, Dad.* That's what I want to tell him. *This isn't funny, and*

I want to talk to Mom.

Now.

He points to the picture in the hot-pink album. "This was taken the day after graduation."

I shake my head, forgetting that each time I move my brain feels like it's getting slammed into ice picks the size of dinosaur claws. "That's next week." I'm desperate to make him understand. Make myself understand. "Graduation is next week," I repeat. "Today's the class trip. Chris is supposed to be here …"

And then I hear it. A sound I've never heard from my dad in the eighteen years I've been alive. A pained, tortured, tormented sob. "There was an accident," he repeats. "Mimi, I'm so sorry."

I can't take my eyes off the photo. I remember my friends. I know all their names, how long we've known each other. I haven't lost all of my memory. So why don't I recognize the hospital room?

Dad's trying hard to keep his composure. I might be mistaken, but I think I feel his body tremble once from the effort. "You were in the hospital for a week."

"I don't remember any of that," I whisper, wishing my dad was lying, wishing he possessed the kind of sick and twisted sense of humor it would take to prank someone in such a grotesque way. But I know my dad. And I know he's telling me the truth.

13

An accident? Took my memory? Why do I remember my own name? Why do I remember my room? Why do I remember that I was supposed to go on my senior class trip today?

"I need to call Chris," I tell him, and immediately I realize I've once again said the wrong thing. The thing that makes Dad grimace, that makes the raw pain even more evident in his expression.

"You can't," he croaks. I've never heard him talk like this. I wonder if someone my age can die of panic. My heart is racing so fast it's making me even dizzier. I force each gulp of air in deliberately, fearing that if I stop, I'll forget to breathe entirely.

"What do you mean I can't?" Why is Dad telling me this? He may not be Chris's biggest fan in the world, but he knows how much my boyfriend means to me. Knows how much I'd need to talk to him at a time like this. Need to hear his voice.

I have to know what happened. I know Dad's probably worried about giving me too many details too fast and making me feel overwhelmed, but there's no way to feel any more confused than I already do. The only thing that's going to help me now is answers.

Lots of them.

"Tell me what happened," I beg. My voice is whiny. I can't

mask my terror.

"I think you should get dressed. I'll make you breakfast."

What's Dad talking about? Does he seriously think I'd be worrying about my wardrobe or my appetite right now? At the mention of food, my stomach sloshes with nausea. I wonder how fast I can race to my bathroom in my condition if I have to throw up.

"I need to call Chris," I tell him again, glancing around the room, desperate to locate my phone. Tears streak down my cheeks. I can hardly breathe. Is this what it feels like when your body goes into shock? Is the strain going to give me a heart attack? "Where's my phone?"

Dad turns his face away. I can't see his expression. Have no idea what he's thinking, what he's going to say next. A terrible question grips me. What if we've done this before? What if we've had this exact same conversation in the past, only I can't remember it?

I touch Dad's arm. We're not used to being physical with each other. Not in years. But he has to understand what I'm going through. Has to realize that it's the uncertainty that's going to kill me, not the truth itself.

"Please," I repeat, barely able to raise my voice beyond a whisper. "Please tell me what happened. I need to know everything."

CHAPTER 4

Springtime. I've always loved the spring. And today's going to be perfect. Time to get myself up and out of bed.

Mom gives her normal *rat-a-tat-tat* on my bedroom door. I push the covers off and call out, "Come in."

She's full of smiles. Steps over and kisses me on the cheek. "How's my little graduating senior?" she asks in a melodic voice. Usually she's way too cheerful in the morning. It annoys me when she comes in singing songs or making jokes. But not today.

Today, I'm even more of a morning lark than she is.

It's the senior trip today. You have no idea how much begging Mom had to do to convince Dad to let me go. "It's just a reason to skip school and party," he grumbled.

Which is when Mom stepped in and offered the family cabin. It wasn't that far from the campsite where seniors historically spent the weekend before graduation. Besides, everyone in my senior class knows Mom. She'd been the school librarian at the middle school before she started subbing at the high school. Sports jocks, band geeks, computer nerds — at one point she's taught in each and every one of their classes.

And everyone loves her.

"Your mom's like the only adult in the entire world I can trust not to totally ruin our camping trip," Kelsie told me when I asked her what she thought of the plan. "And your cabin is the best. I wish my family was loaded like yours. Benefits of having a mob boss as your dad." We laughed at the little inside joke, and that's how it was settled.

I still can't believe I'll get to spend three full days with my friends. Not everyone from our class is coming. Some of the other cliques organized their own getaways. Senior trips are always like that. It's not an actual school-sponsored event. And I guess Kelsie's right when she tells me how lucky I am to have a mom like mine because it doesn't even weird me out to think about her coming with us. Like I said, everyone at the school already knows her. She'll just read her spy novels the whole time anyway, so it's not like she's going to make things awkward or get in our way.

This will be the first time I've spent the night with Chris. Oh my gosh, I had no idea how bad that would sound. No, it's not going to be like *that*. First of all, my parents would kill me if they found out Chris and I were sleeping together. And Chris is really serious about being a Christian, even though he can't let his dad know or he'd get beat up even more than normal. I actually think that's part of the reason why Chris became a Christian in the first place, just because church gave him someplace to go that wasn't home. It was actually at youth group where we started hanging out more, and we've been together now for a little over three years, so it's pretty serious. But we're still gonna wait to do anything like that, if you know what I mean.

But oh my gosh, I'm so excited for this weekend to start! Let's see, I packed my bags, I've got my bug spray. What else do I need? I guess I'm lucky because if I do forget something, it's not like I can't find it at my own cabin, right?

Chris hasn't ever been there before. I hope he feels comfortable. He'd never say so, but sometimes I worry it makes him feel bad when he sees how much stuff my family has. His mom's been out of the picture for a while, and his dad isn't that good with handling the money he manages to earn. Mom tells me all the time not to make Chris think I feel sorry for him. Last summer, when she found out I was paying for our snacks and things whenever Chris and I went out together, she talked Dad into hiring him to do some landscaping. Said that it would make Chris feel better if he didn't think he was relying on our charity.

I guess maybe some people are sensitive about that kind of thing, but Chris and I haven't ever talked about it directly. He did like working at our house last summer, and I'm glad he'll be doing it again this year.

I still can't believe we're almost graduating! And if you want to know a big, deep secret, I'm a little nervous about this camping trip. Because next fall Chris's staying in Massachusetts and taking classes at the community college, and I'm off to New York, and we've never really sat down to talk about what that's going to mean for us. I don't want to be the one to bring it up. I know Chris has enough on his mind already. Did I tell you about his half-sister? Her mom just dropped her off with Chris's dad last year, and so Chris has been basically raising her ever since. That's part of the reason why he wants to stay in the area, I think, to help take care of Gabriella. I don't blame him. I wouldn't trust Mr. Gomez to look after a hamster, much less a little girl.

Well, Mom's in the kitchen now, still singing. I wonder what's for breakfast. Chris will be here in about half an hour, then Mom will drive us over to the cabin. The rest of the group will meet us in the afternoon. We're leaving early so we can do a little grocery shopping once we get there, make sure there's enough food. Mom's pretty strict about no drinking (which is another reason we have a smaller group than we might have),

19

but that's fine by us. Most of Chris's and my crowd isn't into that kind of stuff anyway. And Dad would totally flip if he thought there was going to be anything like that going on.

"You look just like a summer sunflower," Mom tells me when I come out of my room. It's sweet of her to say but kind of silly seeing as how I'm just wearing some plain old cutoff shorts and a yellow striped shirt. She comes over and messes with the clip in my hair, pulling some runaway strands away from my face. Then she gives me a kiss. "Want some coffee with breakfast?" she asks, but I tell her no thanks.

"Dad already at work?" I ask, and she tells me he is. I shouldn't feel surprised. Dad's never here when I get up in the morning. But for some reason I was hoping that today might be different.

Mom must sense the hint of a gloomy mood, and she gives me another huge hug. "I still can't believe you're graduating!" Sometimes, I think she's more excited about me finishing high school than I am. I mean, the way she's going at it, you'd think I'd already discovered the cure for cancer.

We sit down at the table. Mom's made a big breakfast this morning, way more than the two of us could possibly eat. I know why she's done it too, because then when Chris comes by, she can tell him we have extra. He'll never admit when he's hungry or if they're out of food in his house. Mom's gotten into the habit of buying a few extra boxes of snacks from the clearance shelves. It's not the kind of stuff our family ever eats, so she'll tell Chris something like, "You know what? I was cleaning out the back of the pantry and found some things that are about to go bad. Want to take them home?" And he always does. A few times, Mom has tried to figure out what kind of snacks Gabriella likes the most, and she'll always buy a couple extra boxes if she comes across them.

"So, are you going to miss high school?" Mom asks.

I shrug. "It'll be different."

"You're going to love New York," she gushes, and I know she's right. One other cool thing is that Kelsie's been accepted to Barnard, so we'll be practically neighbors. Mom's warned me plenty of times that even though Kelsie and I have been best friends forever, that doesn't mean we'll stay close in college, but I know we will. That's just the kind of friendship we have.

Mom stares at me picking at my fruit salad. "What's wrong? Is the watermelon too mushy? I was a little worried when I cut it up."

I give her a smile. She knows I'm not thinking about the fruit, and she knows that I know.

She reaches over and puts her hand on my knee. "This is going to be a special weekend for you and Chris, isn't it?"

I spear a slice of kiwi and stare at my fork.

"You're a lucky girl," Mom tells me. "That boy loves you very much. I must have taught you how to pick well."

We chuckle, our shared laugh breaking a little bit of the tension I'm feeling at the thought of this senior trip and everything it means. The last time we'll be together like this, me and all my friends ... As much as I want to fight it, I know Mom's right. Graduation means everything's going to change. Kelsie and I will still be best friends, but it's not like we're going to be able to schedule all of our classes together and eat lunch at the same table and spend every free minute together. And Chris ...

The doorbell rings. He's here early. Mom eyes my plate. "Want me to let him in?"

I jump up from my chair. "No, I got it."

I forget how many times Mom and I both have told Chris he can just walk in and make himself at home, but I actually think it's adorable how he still uses the doorbell and stands patiently on the porch.

I open the door. He's wearing his Vegas shirt. Chris and I have been fans of the band since Mom got us tickets to their concert last fall.

"Come in," Mom says, then reminds Chris he doesn't have

to use the bell. It's a conversation they go through every time he comes over. Some things never change. At least I hope they'll never change.

I give Chris a quick hug. He's always shy to be affectionate with me around my parents. If my dad were here, I'd totally get it, but I wish Chris would learn to be a little more comfortable with Mom. In a way though, it just makes him that much more endearing. It's not like he has to be nervous or reserved around Mom either. She absolutely adores him. Says he reminds her of Captain America, all polite and respectful. It makes me happy to know she likes him so much.

I take his hand and give it a squeeze. "Want some breakfast?" I ask. "We just sat down."

It takes less coaxing than usual to get Chris to eat, and he lets Mom pile up his plate without protesting. Good old Chris.

"You two ready for a great weekend or what?" Mom asks, and Chris and I glance at each other. Does he look nervous? Is he wondering the same thing I am?

Is this weekend going to be the beginning of a new stage in our relationship?

Or will it be a bittersweet ending to the best years of our lives?

CHAPTER 5

I'm still crying, but not quite as hysterically. Dad's changed my coffee out for a mug of tea, and we're sitting in the living room now. I look around me, and I recognize everything. I know everything. The bookshelves lined with Mom's mysteries and thrillers, the hundreds of worn paperbacks she's picked up from library sales and thrift stores. The mantle with a few of my gymnastics trophies from days gone by. My brother Marco's wrestling medal from back when he was in high school.

I know this room, this house. Nothing has changed, but everything is different. Dad sees me shivering and goes into my room, bringing out the same pink bedspread I've slept with for years. He tucks it around me like Mom used to do when I stayed home sick from school, watching TV all day on this exact couch. I have so many questions swirling around in my brain I don't even know where to start.

Dad sits in his recliner, the same recliner he's always sat in.

I remember the time I spilled salsa on it and was so scared he'd be mad at me, but he'd laughed and said they'd paid for extra treatment on the leather to make it stain proof. This room, this house, is full of memories. Dad tells me I hit my head. It happened on the senior camping trip, the one I could have sworn was supposed to start today.

"Short-term memory loss," he explains. And just as clearly as I know my own name, I know what he's going to say next. *Like Dory from* Finding Nemo.

"Like Dory from *Finding Nemo*," he adds, as if on cue.

I was right. We've done this before, Dad and me. I remember.

Or do I?

"Can it be fixed?" Maybe I've asked this question before too.

Dad stares at my feet. "We hope so, baby. We hope so." He gets up and hands me some pain meds. I hope they start working soon.

I reach my hand up. Touch the back of my skull where it hurts the most. "I can't feel anything there," I say. It surprises me. An injury that serious — shouldn't there be a bump or something?

Dad lets out a heavy sigh. "You've had a long road to recovery. For the first few weeks, you didn't even know who I was."

Wait a minute. The first few *weeks*? Maybe I heard wrong. Maybe the injury messed up my ears, too. That has to explain it.

"How long have I been like this?" I don't really want to know, but I remind myself that the truth couldn't hurt more than the uncertainty.

Right?

Dad doesn't seem to want to answer. I lean in toward him and repeat, "How long have I been like this?"

He clears his throat. He still isn't looking at me. "Three months."

Now I'm sure my hearing's been affected too. "Months?" I think I'm raising my voice. If I'm not, I should be. I try to get up, but Dad's already standing over me, keeping me on the couch, and I wonder again, *How many times have we gone through this before?*

My eyes are spilling over with tears. So are his, except this time he doesn't try to hide them.

"Months?" I repeat in disbelief, my voice nothing more than a pitiful squeak.

"I'm so sorry, Mimi." He leans down and hugs me. A real hug, not just the arm and shoulder pats we'd grown used to.

"I'm so, so sorry."

I'm crying, but it doesn't even feel like me anymore. Maybe I'm not me at all. How can you be yourself when you've forgotten half of the things that made you you?

Dad's stroking my hair. The gesture reminds me of something. Reminds me of someone. Can the truth be any worse than not knowing?

I'm about to find out.

I steady my breath. Pull away enough that I can look Dad right in the face. Because I may have forgotten my best friend visiting me in a hospital room. I may have forgotten my senior camping trip and this accident Dad keeps talking about.

But I haven't forgotten my family and how much they love me. How they would never leave me alone at a time like this. Which only means one thing.

Do I want the truth? I'm not sure. But I need to find out.

"Where's Mom?" I demand. "Why isn't she here?"

CHAPTER 6

"Mimi," Dad says, trying to coax me, "I need you to calm down. Mom can't be here right now."

"Liar!" I shout. I may have forgotten whatever happened that gave me this freakish headache and turned me into a person I don't even know anymore, but I certainly haven't forgotten my mother. And nothing would keep her from being here with me. Nothing at all.

"Calm down, baby." Dad's smothering me. I kick and fling my body. I may not remember my senior trip, but I know that he wouldn't really hurt me. So I fight back. He can't subdue me this easily.

"Mimi, please." He's begging. Pleading. But I don't care. He owes me answers. He owes me an explanation. And if he thinks that I'm going to calm myself down before he tells me what happened …

The doorbell rings. We both stop struggling. Straighten ourselves up as if it's written out for us on some script. I tidy

28

up the couch cushions that fell askew in our skirmish. Dad goes to the door.

"Detective Drisklay." I can tell from Dad's voice he isn't happy for the intrusion. The name Drisklay does nothing to jog my defective memory, but my brain latches onto the word *detective.*

"Who's here?" I call out, afraid that Dad might send this stranger on his way. I want this detective to know I'm here. "Who is it?" I call out again.

I hear a mumbled response from the foyer, then the sound of the door clicking shut. I strain. Two sets of footsteps are coming toward the living room.

"Mia," Dad says, his face taut, his expression set, "this is Detective Drisklay. He's got some questions for you if you feel up to it."

Do I feel up to it? Absolutely. Because I've got questions of my own.

"Can I get you a drink, Detective?" Dad's voice isn't warm and hospitable like Mom's would be. In fact, there's a hint of cold irony in his tone.

Detective Drisklay holds up a Styrofoam cup. "Brought my own." He sits down in Dad's recliner. I'm surprised that Dad doesn't ask him to move but instead remains standing, his arms crossed.

The detective doesn't even glance over at him but fixes his eyes on me. "How are you feeling today?"

There's a familiarity to his tone that makes me wonder if he's met me before.

"We've had a little bit of a rough morning," Dad interjects, but the detective doesn't take his eyes off mine.

Drisklay sets his Styrofoam cup on our coffee table and pulls out a little notebook from his breast pocket. "Mind if I ask you a couple questions? It'd really help us with our investigation."

Dad takes a step forward. "I haven't had the chance to tell her yet. She still doesn't know."

Drisklay continues to frown. Continues to ignore my dad. I look to my father. A minute ago, I was literally beating against his chest, pleading for answers. Now I just want him to swoop in and carry me to my bed and tuck me in with the promise that this is all some sort of terrible dream. I don't like this Drisklay guy, don't like his hardened scowl or his gravelly voice. Everything about him is harsh. Like a sharpened tack or a rusty nail.

I don't know who he is or what he's doing here, but I want him out of my house.

Now.

Drisklay scribbles something in his notebook then glances up at me like I'm some sort of test rat or science experiment gone wrong. If he knows about my story, if he knows what I've been through, I'd expect at least some slight hint of compassion in his expression, but his face is made of granite, and I hate him.

Dad takes a step closer to me. Instinctively I reach out and grab his hand. I'm trembling, even though I don't know why.

"I told you," Dad tells the detective tersely, "this isn't going to get you anywhere. She doesn't remember."

Drisklay clears his throat. I've never seen anyone ignore my dad the way the detective does.

"I'm sorry you've had a rough morning, Miss Blanca." There's something about the way he says my name. Something slimy. When this detective guy goes away, I want to take a shower. I feel exposed. Filthy. Maybe after he leaves, I'll forget him entirely. Worse things could happen, right?

The detective leans forward. Stares right at me. "So. What can you tell me about the night of May 24?"

He repeats the question once more before I'm crying again. I feel like a baby, but I can't help it. "I don't remember anything. Why do you keep asking me?"

The detective's only been here a few minutes, but long enough that I feel even more confused and terrified than before. In a childish fit, I want to yell at Dad and tell him to kick this guy out of our home. My memory's broken. That's what Dad told me. Something happened at the cabin. Something that stole so much of what I took for granted. The detective wants me to remember, but Dad hasn't told me anything. I just want to know where Mom is. That's the only thing that could even begin to fix this. Seeing Mom, falling into her arms, hearing her promise me that everything's going to be all right.

"The night of May 24," Drisklay repeats, only increasing my hatred toward him. "What can you tell me?"

"Nothing. I don't remember anything."

Dad's sitting next to me on the couch, and I cling to him. My breath comes in short, choppy bursts. How can I tell these two men that the only thing I want in the world is my mother?

Finally, Drisklay lets out a long sigh. "I want to help you, Miss Blanca." I wish he'd stop calling me that. I want to scream every time he says it. "But I can't help you until you tell me the truth. The doctors said your memory should have recovered by now ..."

"Well, obviously it didn't," Dad interrupts, taking a step toward the detective.

Drisklay finally takes the hint and stands up. "Well, call me when that changes," he says. "Our investigation depends on it."

Dad gives him another one of those sarcastic sneers. "Trust me, when Mia recovers, you'll be the first to know."

CHAPTER 7

Dad doesn't listen when I insist that I'm not hungry. Finally, I'm so exhausted from arguing with him that I give in, and he pours me a bowl of cereal.

I don't bother to ask where Mom is. There are so many things I need to figure out.

"I have some work to do," Dad says. "I'll be in the office if you need anything."

It's the first time he's mentioned that all-precious job of his, and somehow knowing that he's still focused on something else outside of whatever trauma's going on in my brain gives me a sense of relief. If I was in that bad of shape, he wouldn't be thinking about work at all.

Would he?

Dad walks down the hall, up the stairs past the foyer, and when I hear the door to his home office click shut, I jump up from my chair. After tossing my soggy cereal into the sink, I sprint toward my room. It's more like a stumble, truth be told, but my body is surging with enough adrenaline that I may as well be racing for my life.

Inside my room, I yank open my drawers. Where is my cell phone? I tear around the place blindly. If I can't find my phone, what else is there to look for? I've never been one to keep a diary. Too risky when you have an older brother who'd love nothing more than to read your most revealing secrets and lord them over you. I scan my bookshelves. Yearbooks? Nothing. Not even the photographs of Chris I had pinned up on my bulletin board. Come to think of it, even my bulletin board is gone now. What's happening to me?

In a desk drawer, I find the Bible my mom gave me when I started junior high. A Teen Study Bible. I still remember how old and mature I felt, having something with *teen* written right there on the front cover. I flip open to a random page.

Remember when you're choosing your friends that the Bible says, "Bad company corrupts good character."

The short devotional goes on to tell me that if I constantly hang out with kids who make bad decisions, I might end up falling into temptation as well. I slam the book shut. Hard to accept advice on making friends when have no idea where all mine are.

Three months. Dad says I've been like this for three months.

That means it's what? The end of August?

What about NYU? What about my scholarship?

I glance down at the Bible again, the little devotional mocking me. Friends? Where are my friends? Has Kelsie gone to Barnard already? Has she left me?

And where is Chris? If he knew how sick I was, if he knew what happened to me, he'd be here.

I need my phone. Kelsie will tell me what happened. She won't treat me like I'm fragile or broken. She'll tell me exactly what I need to know. And Chris will comfort me. Promise me that he's here for me no matter what.

I need to talk to my boyfriend. He must be so worried about me. Where is my stupid phone? If I could just find it, everything could go back to normal ...

I'm banging open drawers, dumping items across the floor.

"What in the world is going on in here?" Dad appears in my doorway, and I immediately feel guilty. I don't know what to tell him.

"I just wanted to find my phone." It's the best I can do, but it does nothing to convey what I'm feeling. What I'm really looking for. Clues. Answers. My identity. I don't mean to start crying again but I do. Maybe I'm hormonal. Maybe it's PMS. How would I know when I last had my period if I can't remember the past three months?

Thinking about all I missed only makes my headache worse. Dad's holding his office phone. Probably has whoever he's been talking to on mute. "Listen," he says, "I've got to finish this call, and then we'll talk, okay?"

I sniff. Knowing my dad, "finishing this call" could take another four hours. At least while he's engrossed in work, I can try to figure things out on my own. I'll just have to do it more quietly.

I put on a smile to placate him. "Okay," I say. "I'll be ready whenever you are."

CHAPTER 8

Half an hour later and I've made three important discoveries.

One: My cell phone is no longer in existence. Either that or it's turned off or something. I've called it from our landline and stood around waiting in every single room of the house and didn't hear it ring once. Which means it's either tucked away in Dad's office, it's on silent, or it simply vanished.

Just like my memory.

Of course, without my cell, I don't know anybody's phone number. Can't call Chris on our home phone because his information is stuck in the contacts section of my non-existent cell.

But that's not the only thing that's missing from around here, which leads me to discovery number two: Besides what Dad showed me this morning in that album, there isn't a single photograph in this entire house. Which is pretty telling, seeing how much scrapbooking Mom loves to do. She wanted it to be a surprise, but I know she was making me a memory book to give to me as a graduation gift.

Memory book. Ironic, isn't it?

I know all the places where Mom used to keep her photographs. In cute little storage boxes by the printer in the craft room. On the top shelf of her closet next to her hats.

There's nothing left.

I know that photos don't just disappear. They're saved on hard drives, saved to the cloud, saved on Mom's Facebook page. I turn on the computer in the spare bedroom, and guess what? Somebody's changed all the passwords. I try everything. Dad's birthday. Mom's birthday. My birthday. I remember everything so clearly. The names of my various goldfish growing up.

Nothing works.

So here I am. No memory, or at least missing a huge three-month chunk. No way to look up anything on my phone or the family computers. No pictures of Chris or anything else for that matter. Think. What do I need to do?

The landline. I still have the landline. But what good is that if I don't have anybody's phone number memorized? I walk back downstairs. I have to go slowly because I'm still dizzy. My stomach is empty, but I'm too nauseated to eat.

Back in the kitchen. Staring at the landline phone. What

could I do? I know Mom's cell number, at least. It's …

It's …

Wait, I know it. I know I do.

Mom's number. When I was younger and she needed help locating her lost cell, she'd shout out the numbers for me to dial into the landline. I scan the room. There must be something to jog my memory. Some sort of trigger. When Mom lost her cell, she'd tell me to call it. She'd say the numbers were …

I know there's a 2. There's a 2 and a 7. Wait, now that jingle from the pizza delivery commercial is in my head. Dang it. Why can't I focus?

My eyes dart around wildly until they land on the fridge. That's it. When Marco and I were little and Mom hired a babysitter, she always kept emergency numbers on the fridge.

I've got the landline in my hand and ignore the fact that I'm shaking. *Check the fridge. Check the fridge.*

Magnets Dad brought home when he went on business trips and Marco and I were young enough to still expect trinkets as gifts. The same flowery notepad Mom always buys from the craft store to keep track of menu planning and grocery lists, except it's totally blank. A magnet with the contact info for some banker Dad works with. Not going to be any help.

No emergency numbers.

Wait.

There's something down there between the fridge and the stove. It must have fallen. If I could twist my arm a certain way, I might just be able to reach ...

My heart is racing. I need those numbers. My fingers brush against the side of the fallen magnet.

No. I've pushed it back even farther now. I glance toward the hallway, where I'm certain Dad's going to appear any minute, demanding to know what I'm doing. If my arm was just another inch longer ...

I grab one of Mom's wooden spoons. See if I can scrape the magnet against the floor, drag it closer to me.

I've got it. It's ...

My hands tremble as I stare at the words. *Angelo's. We Deliver.* A local telephone number that isn't going to help me do anything except order a pizza.

The doorbell rings. I'm not going to wait for Dad to come out of his office or tell me whether I should answer it or not. Right now, even if it's that nasty detective from earlier this morning, I don't care. I just need to talk with someone who can explain exactly what's going on.

I march toward the doorway, ignoring the dizziness. Ignoring the shaking in my body.

It's time for me to get some answers.

CHAPTER 9

"Mia, how good to see you." The woman standing on my porch steps in and wraps me up in a giant hug. "How are you, dear? You remember me, don't you?" She lets out a chuckle. I'm not sure what's so funny, but I'm relieved to say that yes, I do know her.

"Is your Dad home?" she asks.

I nod. "He's in his office. Doing some work."

Sandy gives me a smile and steps into the foyer. I've known her for years. Her husband's the pastor at our church, and she ran one of the teen girls Bible studies I used to belong to.

"Well, I don't know if you remember this," Sandy says, "but I've been coming over here every Tuesday to pray with you and talk through anything you might want to chat about."

Good. This is better than some emergency number written out on the fridge. Sandy can actually help me. Can actually fill in the three months I've lost.

I follow Sandy into our sitting room, and she makes herself

at home. I have to wonder how many times we've done this. Every Tuesday?

"How's your head today?" Sandy looks perfectly comfortable and content sitting there, as if she were a queen residing over her adoring followers.

"Hurts," I answer truthfully.

"So you talked to your father this morning?" Sandy asks.

I nod. "Yeah. A little bit. There was a detective here too."

"Officer Drisklay?" I can't tell by Sandy's voice what she thinks of him, but given how unpleasant my own experience was, I wonder if she dislikes him as much as I do. "How did that go?" she asks kindly.

I shrug. "I don't really know."

I'm not sure what to expect. Even though I was in Sandy's Bible study for a few years, this is the first time we've talked one-on-one. At least, this is the first time that I remember us talking one-on-one. It feels weird. Like maybe the pastor's wife at such a big church has other things to be doing. Our family isn't even all that active there.

Sandy clears her throat. "Did your dad show you the photo album?"

I nod, wondering how many times Sandy and I have had this exact same conversation in the past three months.

"I'm guessing you still don't remember what happened?" There's something in the way Sandy says it. Something gentle in her voice. I find myself getting more comfortable, if only just a little.

"It's hard to ..." I raise my hand to the back of my skull, not sure if my head hurts worse than it did before or if I'm just focused on the pain now that we're talking about my memory.

"I know it's disorienting." Sandy's voice is so soft. Her features so maternal. "If there's anything I can do ..."

I don't know how much longer Dad's going to be up in his office, but I'm not about to let this opportunity pass me up. I lean forward, stare intently into Sandy's kind eyes, and blurt out, "Can you tell me where my mom is?"

Sandy shifts in her seat on the couch. She doesn't look uncomfortable. Not exactly. And if my question caught her off guard, she doesn't show it. Still, there's something in her expression I can't quite place.

"Your dad hasn't told you yet?"

I shake my head, and for a split second I wonder if I really want to know.

Sandy has my hand in hers. We're sitting so close our knees almost touch. She presses her lips together. "Are you sure you're ready for me to tell you?"

"Please," I beg. "I need to know."

This seems to be the answer she was waiting for. Sandy sighs. Gives my hand a squeeze. "Sweetie, I'm so sorry that I have to be the one to tell you this. No matter how many times you hear it, I know it never gets any easier."

This is torture. Like being a little kid watching the nurse prepare your injection, where waiting is worse than the pain itself.

Sandy shakes her head. Clucks her tongue. "Pumpkin," she says, "I want you to listen to me very carefully. This isn't going to be easy for you to hear."

Just tell me, I want to shout, but somehow, with everything else I've forgotten how to do, I can't remember how to talk. Not right now. It's taking all of my energy just to breathe.

"Mia." Sandy's voice is pained. Full of compassion. "Your mother passed away, sweetie. She's with Jesus now."

CHAPTER 10

I'm snuggled against Chris in the backseat of the minivan. Mom says that's fine, that she has a new playlist she's been dying to listen to anyway. I think she knows Chris and I need this time. This privacy.

She taps a few buttons on her phone and makes a show of tuning into her soft rock mix station, turning the volume up as high as it will go. Giving me one quick glance in the rearview mirror, she flashes me a smile before pulling on her sunglasses and backing out of our driveway.

I glance up at Chris. I'm sitting in the middle seat since Mom's packed the cooler right next to me. Maybe she did it because she knows how much I like to be next to the people I'm closest to. It's my love language, she tells me. Physical touch.

I give Chris a little nudge with my shoulder. "Well, what do you think?"

"About what?" he asks with a grin.

"About the weekend," I answer. We're both whispering,

even though so far we haven't said anything we'd be embarrassed for Mom to hear. "Senior trip. Can you believe it?"

"No. I can't." There's a faraway look in Chris's eyes. I didn't mean to turn the conversation so serious so soon. I try to change the subject.

"You ready for the history final?" I ask.

"Yeah. Thanks to you." Chris and I have spent the past couple weeks studying together. He has to pass in order to graduate.

"Want me to quiz you?" I offer.

"Nah. It's nice just sitting back here." His voice gets a little wistful. It's the tone he gets when he's thinking.

I don't ask too much about Chris's home life. He tells me some. More, I think, than he ever wanted anybody to know. But with secrets like that, it's not healthy to keep them to yourself. I'm glad he came to me. Glad he trusted me. But it's not like it's something we talk about every single time we get together. He knows I'm here if he needs me, and that's good enough for both of us.

I've actually never been to Chris's house. Not in the entire three years we've been dating. I've seen his dad once or twice but never spoken to him. It's a sad family life. There's no denying that. It's miraculous that Chris has turned out so normal. I know a ton of that is because he started going to youth group and got serious about his faith. I sometimes feel like he's disappointed in me that I'm not as spiritual as he is. I don't mean to say we're totally different. I believe in God just as much as he does. Chris is just more open about talking about things like that, whereas I keep my faith more private. More personal.

I reach out and grab Chris's hand then lean my head against his chest. He's strong. I feel so safe here. I start playing with his thumb, drawing little patterns on it with my own, clicking on the nail that's so much thicker and stronger than mine. In a moment of impulsivity, I bring his hand up toward my face and kiss one of his knuckles.

"What was that for?" he asks sheepishly.

"For being you."

We ride without having to speak. It's nice. We have a little over two hours. No rush to get out a lot of words right now. No rush to dive into the discussions neither of us is ready to have. Like what will happen to us once we graduate and I go off to New York and he stays here.

I've thought about deferred admissions, even though I haven't told my parents. Mom would understand, but Dad would probably throw a fit. There's nothing that says I couldn't start at NYU next year. I could even save money taking a few classes locally.

And of course, I'd be closer to Chris ...

Part of me feels like he should be the one to bring these things up, but I know he'd never ask me to do something like that. To give up my scholarship just to stay by him.

This is a decision I'll have to make on my own.

He's got his arm around my shoulder, which is sweet. It also shows how much more comfortable he's grown around my mom. A year ago, he would have never dared to sit like this if anybody in my family was around. Chris and my mom get along great, but of course there's not a single person in the world my mom can't win over. I'll admit, Dad can be kind of intense, so I don't blame Chris for acting nervous when he's around. Chris doesn't really know what it's like to have a father who doesn't beat you up when he's angry, so there's that too. I think Chris and Marco would get along pretty well, but my brother's busy selling pharmaceuticals. He's hardly ever around anymore, and he's only met Chris once or twice. Still, they've been cordial enough with each other. I think there's potential there at least.

"I love you," I whisper, wrapping my arms around his waist.

Chris glances nervously at my mom in the driver's seat.

"Don't worry," I tell him, "it's not like it's that big of a secret." I laugh and feel his body relax.

"I love you," I repeat and wonder if I'll ever be happier than I am right now.

I don't know what the future has in store for Chris and me. Maybe I'll stay around with him for another year and we'll grow even closer than we already are. Or maybe we'll find that when I'm in New York, the distance only makes our relationship that much stronger.

All I know is that this is the happiest I've ever felt, right now. Right at this moment.

A moment I know I'll never forget.

CHAPTER 11

I blink. *Passed away*? *With Jesus*? What in the world is Sandy talking about?

"I'm sorry," she repeats. "Come here." She wraps me up in a hug. A hug that feels more familiar than I think it should. I remember what she told me. *Every Tuesday*. If my head didn't hurt so much, I could try to do the math. Guess how many times Sandy's told me this same news, how many hugs just like this she's given.

Should I cry? Part of me thinks I should cry. Have I already spent my daily allotment of tears? Am I a terrible person? Shouldn't I be throwing myself on the couch, pounding the pillows, telling Sandy it can't be true?

That's probably the reaction Sandy was expecting. Maybe she thinks I'm in shock or numb and that's why she's still holding me and petting my head like I'm some kind of lap dog in need of comfort.

No, it's different than that. I've been in shock before. How else would you describe what you experience when you wake up and realize that three months of your life, entire chunks of your brain, are missing?

This isn't shock.

In fact, my head feels clearer and more focused than it has all day.

I begged Sandy to tell me what happened to my mom, and she did. Except I know something she doesn't. That's why I'm not crying. That's why I'm not panicked or hysterical.

I don't remember what happened. I don't have a clue where Mom is or why Sandy is gripping me so tightly that suddenly I feel like I'm the one who's meant to comfort her.

I don't feel confused, sad, or scared. I know my memory's missing. I can't explain why all the photographs in our home have been removed or why I can't find my cell or log into any of the computers.

But I do know one thing.

Mom isn't dead. I'm not in shock or denial. In fact, I'm thinking more clearly than I've been since I woke up this morning.

Mom isn't dead. Which means that somebody is lying to me.

I don't know Sandy as well as I could. Like I said, our family hasn't been the most regular of attenders at her church, and I stopped going to her girls' Bible study a couple years ago when life got too busy.

But I know that Sandy would never intentionally lie to anybody. And I know by the way she's working so hard to comfort me that she honestly believes my mom is dead.

Sandy isn't lying to me. Not deliberately.

Which means that somebody else is.

And I think I know who that might be.

CHAPTER 12

I need to be careful to play this right. Need to be careful to make sure Sandy thinks I'm upset without going so overboard she sees right through me.

I muster up a few tears. Nothing over the top. She still hasn't let me go from her wrestler-strength hug, so I just need to shake my shoulders some and make a few small sobbing sounds. Sandy really is crying, which makes me feel guilty. Like I'm tricking her or something. The truth is I just need to figure out what Sandy knows, or what she thinks she knows.

Mom isn't dead. This isn't wishful thinking. I *know* it. I remember something … I have no idea what it is, but if I can get Sandy to keep talking, I'll figure it out. I have to.

"What happened?" I keep my voice small and force a little tremor.

Sandy gives me one last squeeze then pulls away. "I think you should probably ask your dad about that."

I shake my head, trying hard not to let her guess that Dad is the very last person I'd trust to tell me the truth right now. "I want to hear it from you," I state.

Sandy heaves a sigh. She's still holding my hand in hers. I give it a squeeze and try to look both thankful and needy.

"Well," Sandy begins, "do you remember your senior trip?" I nod. I don't have time for her to fill me in on inconsequential details. Who knows how long we'll have to talk in private, just the two of us? So I pretend to recall more than I do. "We went to the cabin," I answer. "Mom drove Chris and me."

When I say Chris's name, something in Sandy's expression changes. It's slight. Hardly noticeable. Except I do notice.

Sandy straightens out her flowery skirt, focusing for a few seconds on one of its more prominent wrinkles. "Do you remember what happened once you got there?"

"We got things ready and waited for the rest of the group to show up." I don't know if I'm just making an educated guess or relying on some sort of latent memory that remains locked up in my brain.

"It happened right before noon."

I lean forward. There's something familiar about Sandy's words. I remember. I ... I think I remember.

Maybe I remember remembering?

I have to focus. Need to pay attention to each syllable she speaks.

"You were …" Sandy's voice falters. "You were attacked, sweetie. You and your mom both."

I pretend to give a little cry. Pretend like I'm absorbing this information for the first time. But I know that I remember something. Do I just remember Sandy telling me this same story before, or is there more to it than that? If I could just clear up this stupid headache …

I need more pain meds or something, but I can't stop right now. I have to play the part. Have to act like the girl who's just found out her mom has been killed. Sandy believes every word she's speaking. I know she does.

But I don't.

It didn't happen that way.

You don't have to cry, I want to tell Sandy. In a way, I feel like a monster allowing her to grieve over my family like this when I know it didn't happen the way she said it did.

An attack at the cabin. That part doesn't sound familiar. At least I don't think it does. I was attacked. Mom was too …

No, it didn't happen that way.

Which means my mom isn't really dead.

Which means that someone is lying to me. And that same person has lied to Sandy too.

55

A question bursts through the surface of my mental fog. "What about Chris?"

Sandy shakes her head. She looks so pitiable, I feel awful, like I'm the one breaking her heart with my questions. "Maybe we should wait for your dad," she whispers.

"Please." I don't need to pretend to beg. Don't need to pretend to act desperate for this information. "I want to hear it from you. Dad never liked Chris to begin with. What happened to him? Please tell me."

Sandy sighs. "Honey, Chris disappeared. He took off, and the police still haven't found him yet."

This comes as a surprise. "Was he kidnapped or something?" My heart is racing. This wasn't what I was expecting Sandy to tell me.

She's hugging me again. What is that smell? Some kind of flowery perfume. Or maybe it's her shampoo. The scent is nauseating and makes my headache even worse.

"Sweetie, this isn't going to be easy for you to hear," Sandy says. "But the police believe Chris was the one who attacked you."

CHAPTER 13

"I don't believe you." I'm irrational. None of this is her fault, but I'm consumed with an inexplicable hatred for Sandy. For her lies.

"You're wrong," I insist. "That's not what happened."

This isn't like me. One second I'm starting to figure it out, feel like I'm actually starting to remember. And then this? I don't know why I'm so angry at her either, but it's not like there's some sort of textbook to tell you how you'll respond when someone comes in and cuts out three whole months of your life.

It makes absolutely no sense at all.

"Chris would have never done this to me," I repeat, and Sandy's holding me, letting me swat at her with my fists. I'm not trying to hurt her. At least I don't think I am. It's a little bit hard to think right now, so excuse me if I'm not acting like myself. As if I even know who that is anymore.

"I know it's hard to hear, sweetie." Sandy keeps repeating

these silly phrases that I'm sure mean well but only sound like nonsense to me. *It's hard to hear?* I'd like to see what she's like after someone opens up her brain and dissects her memories and then tells her that the two people she loves most in the world are actually a murderer and his victim.

It's not true. None of it. Mom's not dead. Chris isn't guilty. Which means he's still out there.

Maybe.

I've got to find him. Is that why Dad took my phone away? And what about Mom? If she's not dead, that means she's somewhere too. Up until today, I thought the worst pain I'd ever been in was when I got my wisdom teeth yanked out. I wish I could go back to that now. I've heard of throbbing headaches before, but at least with a throb there's that pulse of relief, however short lived. The pain for me is constant. Unabated.

I need my mom.

"I didn't want to have to tell you," Sandy sighs, as if this were all my fault. I just wanted answers. I didn't ask for these lies.

"Can I pray for you, sweetie?" she asks, but I shake my head. I know it's probably sinful for me to say, but I can't withstand the mental fog long enough to pay attention to any prayer. I don't know what I'm supposed to do now. I want to sleep. I want to die. I want to throw up. Maybe I'll go and do all three at the same time.

"What in the world is going on in here?" Dad comes racing in, then blurts into the phone, "I'm gonna have to call you back." He stops in the threshold of the living room and stares at Sandy. "Oh. Is it Tuesday?"

She nods, and Dad's angry expression softens.

"So you told her?"

Sandy nods again.

Dad hurries over to me. "Baby, I'm so sorry. I know it's not easy to find out about it this way."

"She told me Mom's dead." I want Dad to laugh. To tell me that Sandy is just making things up, but the pain in his expression tells me that he believes her lies as well.

Or at least he acts as if he does.

"I'm so sorry, Mimi."

"It didn't happen," I protest. Because I know it isn't true. At least I think it isn't true. Am I remembering, or am I just refusing to believe the truth?

I don't have the stomach to mention Chris. I sink back on the couch. Dad and Sandy probably assume I'm still upset at finding out about Mom, but my head hurts so much I can hardly think about her right now. Does that make me a terrible person?

Am I selfish that I'm crying for myself and not my mother?

No, because I know she isn't dead. I'm certain of it.

I'm going to get this figured out. I have to.

In the corner of the living room, Dad and Sandy are having a conversation in hushed tones. I catch the words *sleep* and *shock* and *better after a nap*. Sandy tells my dad it's going to get easier.

"It's so hard to see her like this." He's whispering. Probably thinks I can't hear. Maybe they assume I've even fallen asleep. I'm tired enough I probably could. "Every single week," Dad exclaims, and I squeeze my eyes shut. Is this my new Tuesday ritual? To hear about my mother's death all over again?

"Did she ask about him?" Dad asks.

I'm too tired to hear Sandy's answer. Or maybe she's just better at keeping her voice down.

"I don't think we should tell her anymore. Her brother says it might be better to say she's on a trip or something ..."

I only catch the last half of what Sandy says then. *"The truth will set you free."* It's a verse from the Bible. I recognize it even though I couldn't tell you if it's from the Old or New Testament.

The truth will set you free.

As if I needed another reminder of this prison I'm in. A

prison in my own mind.

The truth will set you free ...

Well, then it's time for me to figure out some answers. Learn the real truth for myself.

But first, I need to sleep ...

CHAPTER 14

Springtime. I've always loved the spring. And today's going to be perfect. It's the senior trip today. Time to get myself up and out of bed.

Ow.

I sit up in bed then look at the clock. One? That doesn't make sense. It can't be night. The sun's out. But I'd never sleep in. Not today.

And why does my head hurt so much?

"Mom?" I glance around my room. Something's missing. I guess the clock could be wrong. Where's my phone? That always has the right time, except I can't find it.

"Mom?"

I'm dizzy when I try to get out of bed. I don't understand any of this. What about my senior trip? Mom wouldn't have let me miss it. And what about Chris? He was going to come over hours earlier. We should be at the cabin by now. Everyone else is already there waiting for us.

I open the door to the hallway, blinking. My eyes aren't used to this light. I look down and wonder how I ended up asleep in my clothes.

Oh, no. I'm sick. I'm going to throw up. Got to hurry.

That's so disgusting, but at least I made it to the bathroom on time.

"Mia?"

I scream when the shower curtain pulls open. I ran in here so fast I didn't realize I wasn't alone.

"Don't worry," he says. "It's me." My brother Marco. What is he doing home? He peeks his head out from behind the shower curtain. "Hand me the towel."

I'm too confused to ask any questions, and I simply do what he says.

The next thing I know, Dad is at the door, his phone in one hand. "Everything okay? What's going on?"

"I startled her," Marco says, stepping out of the shower. Even with his towel wrapped around him, I'm a little weirded out to see my brother like this. I keep my eyes on the toilet bowl where I just emptied my stomach.

I still have no idea why either my brother or my dad are home. Marco never stops by anymore, and Dad should be at work. None of this makes sense, and I'm late for my senior trip. "Where's Mom?"

I study the worried expressions that pass from my father to my brother then repeat, "Where's Mom?"

Dad's about to say something but Marco steps forward. "Hey remember, you got kind of sick right before your camping trip. You told Mom she should go so everyone else could have a good time, but you weren't feeling up to making it." He gives a sympathetic frown. "Sorry, Mimi."

It's a nickname he hasn't called me in years, but it doesn't feel as awkward as I would have thought it might to hear it from him again.

"What are you doing home?" I ask.

He smiles then tousles his wet hair. "Mom felt bad about leaving you for the weekend, and Dad's got work to do, so I said I'd come by and keep you company."

"Oh." I guess it makes sense. Funny that I don't remember any of it though.

"How you feeling?" my brother asks.

"My head hurts." I look over to where Dad was standing, except he's gone. Strange. Wasn't he right there just a second ago?

"Yeah, the doctor said it might."

"I went to the doctor?" Suddenly I feel dizzy. Marco reaches out for my arm, steadying me when I nearly lose my balance.

He gives a little chuckle. "You really are out of it, aren't you?" He gives me a smile, then says, "Hey, let me get dressed and then we'll watch a movie. Once you're feeling better, I'll drive you out to the cabin and you can join your class for the rest of the trip."

Something doesn't feel right, but I can't quite place it. Maybe it's the fact that my brother's being so nice to me when we haven't seen much of each other in years.

"So Mom left without me?" It doesn't sound like something she'd do.

"She didn't want to," Marco says, "but you were so worried about everyone else being disappointed that you begged her to go."

"I did?"

Marco laughs again. "That's my little sis. Always so selfless. And humble enough you don't even remember when you've done it."

Pain pulses from between my temples. "What am I sick with anyway?"

Marco shrugs. "Some kind of 24-hour bug. Headaches, vomiting, disorientation. You seriously don't remember Mom taking you to the doctor?"

I shake my head, and he laughs at me again.

"Meet me downstairs," he says, "and I'll find us a good

movie. Just let me get dressed first."

A few minutes later, Marco comes downstairs, drying his hair with a towel. He tosses it onto Dad's recliner then plops down next to me on the couch. "And how's my favorite little sister?"

"My head hurts," I tell him, and I'm not sure if that's because of this 24-hour bug I have or if it's because I feel so disoriented. I remember getting really sick when I was in second or third grade. Turned into scarlet fever. I was at a gymnastics competition, told Mom I didn't feel well, and the next thing I remember I was home taking lukewarm baths and having Mom stick a thermometer under my tongue every half an hour.

"Want some pain meds?" Marco asks. "Doctor says the over-the-counter stuff is fine."

"Yes, please."

He gets up, and I'm surprised at how attentive he's being. It's not as if my brother and I don't get along. We just don't interact much at all. He comes home on holidays, and that's about it. I honestly can't remember the last time he sat down to watch a movie with me.

He hands me two pills and a cup of water. It's tepid, and I wince drinking it down. "Throat hurts," I croak, handing him my cup.

He nods. "Doctor said it might." He sets the glass on the coffee table. He's lucky Mom's at the cabin or she'd rip into him for forgetting to use a coaster. He kicks his shoes up beside the glass, points the remote at the TV, and asks, "Well, Mimi, what are you in the mood to watch?"

CHAPTER 15

Marco's finished nearly the entire pizza, and he keeps asking me if I want a slice. I don't have the heart to tell him that even the smell of it makes me want to puke.

We just finished watching *Ant-Man and the Wasp*. Marco can't believe how behind I am in the Marvel movies. It wasn't bad at all, but with this headache I had a harder time than I should have following the storyline. When I wake up tomorrow, I'm not even sure I'll be able to tell you what it was about.

"I'm tired," I admit when Marco asks how I'm feeling. It's not even night yet, but maybe if I get to bed early, I'll sleep off this bug and take Marco up on his offer to drive me to the cabin in the morning.

The worst part about today, I mean other than missing the first part of my senior trip, is that I don't have my phone. Mom's cell broke, and Dad didn't want her to drive all the way out to the cabin without one, so she took mine. Marco assures me that she's told Chris and all my friends what happened, but I feel so cut off. Right now, everyone's probably on the deck or at the lake. Mom's getting dinner ready, and it's going to be something far more refined than Marco's eleven-dollar-a-box pizza. Everyone's laughing, everyone's having the time of their lives …

I wish I could be there now.

The doorbell rings. "Stay here," Marco tells me. "I'll get it."

The end credits are still rolling, and I wonder if there's going to be one of those extra scenes at the end. It's the only reason I haven't turned the TV off yet. I hear a noise and eventually manage to stumble to my feet. I'm a little hungry but doubt I'll be able to keep anything down.

Marco's talking to someone in the foyer. I stop before I reach the hallway and listen. I know that voice but can't place it right away.

"… wanted to come by and see how she's doing." Oh. Right. It's Sandy from church. The pastor's wife. What is she doing here?

"That's really nice of you," my brother says, "but she's actually asleep right now."

Asleep? No, I'm not.

"Well, I'm glad you've come home," Sandy says. "This has been a hard time for your father. I know he appreciates the extra help."

"That's what I'm here for."

"I guess you heard about what happened earlier today?" Sandy asked. "How she ..."

"Yeah," Marco interrupts. "That's the reason I'm missing work in the middle of the week."

Middle of the week? What's he talking about?

Sandy lets out a sigh that reverberates from the high ceiling. "It's got to be so hard on your dad, first what happened to your mom, now this."

Something seizes in my chest. A flash of clarity that precedes a pulse of pain through my head so intense it feels like my individual hair follicles are shards of glass piercing my skull.

A flash. I see it for just a split second. Come back. Come back. I almost remember ...

Snippets from their conversation flash between my brain. *Middle of the week ... what happened to your mom ...*

And I know.

I see.

I remember.

I remember everything.

"Mimi?" It's Marco. I didn't even hear him in the hallway.

"Mimi. You okay?"

I can't talk. Can't breathe. I think I'm afraid. Afraid of what?

Afraid of who?

I blink. Who's talking to me? Marco?

"Was someone here?" I ask. It's like I've forgotten something. Something important. What was it?

"Sandy from church," he answers. "She heard you were sick and wanted to know if you needed anything."

He's studying me quizzically. Why is he staring at me like that?

"You look awful," he says. "You should have stayed on the couch. Go lie down."

No, I don't think that's what I want to do. I came here for something. Out to the foyer. I was listening to something. I heard …

What was it?

"My head hurts," I tell him.

Marco gives me a smile. "I know. Come on. Let me get you some Tylenol and then we'll watch another movie."

At first my legs don't want to follow him down the hallway. I'm afraid I can't move at all.

He stops and looks behind him. "Coming?"

His voice snaps me out of my confusion, and now I

remember where I am. What's going on.

It's senior skip weekend. I'm sick. Marco's here to take care of me, and if I'm better by tomorrow, he'll drive me to the cabin to join my friends.

I follow him into the living room. A movie sounds like exactly what I need. Something light. Something I've seen before so I don't really need to pay all that much attention. Something funny where I'll get all the jokes even if I'm listening with my eyes shut.

But first, some Tylenol.

CHAPTER 16

I'm asleep on the couch. At least I think I'm asleep on the couch. The strange thing is I can still hear everything going on around me. I know that Marco's here. I know we finished watching *Thirteen Going on Thirty* even though my brother hates romcoms. I know he only watched it to make me feel better, and I fell asleep sometime after Jennifer Garner's *Thriller* dance.

I know Marco watched the sports channel for a while, even though I couldn't tell you what was on. Then the news, and now the TV's off, and he and Dad are in the living room talking.

"See? It's better this way. No crying. No shock. She's sleeping like a baby."

No, I'm not, I want to say, but my brother isn't listening to me. He's talking to Dad.

"What happens if she finds out anyway?" Dad asks.

"Can't be worse than what you've been putting her through every day, can it?"

"I don't know." I've never heard Dad sound so lost. So broken. I want to go and comfort him, tell him I'm fine. Except I can't because I'm asleep. At least my body is, but my brain is alert.

What's going on?

"Look at her," Marco says. "I bet she hasn't slept this well since the accident. And she's had an entire evening where she's been happy. That's got to count for something, right?"

"I suppose."

Their voices trail off. I want them to come back. I want to learn more. What are they talking about? And since when did Marco get so concerned about me and how well I may or may not be sleeping? And when did he and Dad start getting along? Aren't they supposed to hate each other?

I debate whether or not I want to wake up. Wake up and try to find the answers to these questions myself. Or I could just turn off my brain and rest.

Forget about what Marco said.

Forget about my questions.

Forget everything.

And simply sleep.

CHAPTER 17

"Mia!" Mom calls from the back door of the cabin.

I leave my spot next to Chris by the dock and run barefoot toward the cabin. "Yeah?"

"Come in here," Mom says. "I have a question for you."

"Okay," I bound in, ready for a question about the final guest count or food allergies. But when I see Mom's face, I realize this is something far more serious.

"You having a good time so far with Chris?" she begins.

"Yeah." I hesitate, only because she's looking at me so intently. What's going on?

Mom glances out the window as she dries her hands on the kitchen towel. Chris is sitting on the dock, his feet dangling in the water. "What are you guys talking about out there?"

What is this? An interrogation? "Nothing much," I answer. "Why?"

Mom lets out a sigh. "Well, graduation is bringing lots of changes. I just wanted to know if Chris has mentioned any of his future plans to you yet."

"Like going to community college?" I asked. Mom knows all about that. She's the one who urged him to apply and helped him file for financial aid.

Mom is still looking out the window. "He's a good boy," she tells me. "A good man, I should say." As if I didn't already know. I would usually make a joke right about now, but she seems so intent.

"Chris emailed me earlier," she finally says.

I wait. Why didn't either of them mention something sooner?

"Did you know that Chris called your father at his office this morning?"

Chris calling my dad? Why would he do that? He's terrified of the man.

Mom studies me, the towel still in her hands. "Chris didn't mention any of this?"

"No." Now I'm a little worried. What reason in the world does Chris have to talk about anything to my father, and why wouldn't anybody tell me?

Mom reaches over and gives me a hug. "Well, don't let on that I said anything, all right? I just want you to know that I think Chris is wonderful. And you're a smart, bright, capable woman, and whatever decisions you make, I support you a hundred percent."

Another hug.

"I mean that, Mimi." She holds my gaze. "A hundred percent."

"Okay." I return the embrace albeit a little uncertainly. "Thanks." Trying to lighten the mood, I give a little laugh. "Now if it's all right with you, can I go enjoy some time with my boyfriend again?"

"Of course," Mom says, returning my smile even though her eyes don't reflect it. "Why don't you tell Chris to come in? I'm going to run to the store in a minute and I don't want you two by the water alone."

I roll my eyes. Mom is so laid back about just about everything. Water safety is the only area where she is and always will be entirely paranoid.

"Don't give me that look, young lady." She points a finger at me. "You know what happened ..."

"I know, I know," I interrupt. The story of the little boy who stepped on a bad piece of wood on his dock. If he'd survived, I'm pretty sure he'd be older than me by at least a decade, and yet his tragic fate has served as a warning for families in this area for as long as I can remember.

Mom leans over. Gives me a kiss. "I love you, Mia. I love

you so much, and I'm so proud of the young woman you've become."

She's growing mushy now, probably thinking about my upcoming graduation. A few nights ago, I found her in her craft room poring over my baby pictures. She didn't want me to see she'd been crying, but it was pretty obvious. She's never been good at hiding anything.

Especially from me.

"Well, I'm off to the store," Mom says. Just need to get some milk and some eggs …" She's rattling off her grocery list, but I'm not paying attention. I'm busy looking at my boyfriend from the back window. Chris has gotten up from his spot on the dock. His fists are clenched. He looks so assertive, so sure of himself. What changed?

Mom grabs the keys, gives me one last kiss, and heads out through the garage. I watch while my boyfriend strides toward me with a determination I've never seen in him before in my life.

CHAPTER 18

Springtime. I've always loved the spring. And today's going to be perfect. It's the senior trip today. Time to get myself up and out of bed.

Ow.

I reach over to find my phone, knocking my clock off the nightstand in the process. What time is it?

"That you, Mia?"

Marco? What's he doing home? Ever since he started working for that pharmaceutical company, he's been too busy to ever come by. That and the fact that he and Dad hate each other.

There's a soft knock on my door, and he lets himself in. "You okay?"

"Yeah." I try to sit up, surprised to discover that I'm dizzy. "What's going on?"

"I'm home for the weekend," he says then adds, "Doctor's orders," while flashing me a grin. Doctor's orders? What's that supposed to mean?

"Headache?" he asks, holding out two pills and a cup of water.

"Yeah. How'd you know?"

"You were kind of out of it yesterday," he says. "I thought you might wake up a little groggy, so I wanted to be ready."

"Where's Mom?"

He lets out a chuckle. "What do you mean where's Mom? She went to the cabin."

"For the trip?" That doesn't make any sense. I'm supposed to be there. I'm supposed to be on that class trip. Mom would have never left without me.

Marco takes the cup back and sets it on my end table. "Mom wanted to stay here and take care of you, but you said it'd be better if she went so at least the rest of your friends could have a good time." He waits for the words to sink in. "You really don't remember?"

I shake my head, and he laughs once more. "Well, what'd I always tell you about all that studying you do? You finally went and rotted your brain. Want to get up? I can make you some breakfast. How's French toast sound?"

I'm still trying to get past the part in the conversation where he told me Mom went to the cabin on my senior trip without

"What day is it?" I ask.

"Saturday," he answers. "I told Mom if you were feeling better by this afternoon, I'd drive you up to the lake myself. Why don't you get up? Maybe you just need a little breakfast. Meet me in the kitchen when you're ready."

He shuts my bedroom door behind him, and I sit blinking. I missed my senior trip? Wouldn't I remember that? Every time I move, my head aches. Maybe I really am sicker than I thought. Marco said something about breakfast, but the thought of food sends my stomach swirling in a sea of nausea.

I reach out for my cell phone, then remember that I couldn't find it on my night table just a few seconds earlier. Maybe I knocked it over when I upset the clock. I'd get down on my hands and knees to look for it, but I'm not sure my brain could handle that much jostling. Every time I move my body, it feels like a bolt of lightning is surging through my retinas and burning the back of my skull. I'm so tired. How long have I been asleep?

It takes forever, but I finally manage to get myself dressed and head down the hall. I'm surprised to hear Dad's voice on the phone in his office. What's he doing home? He never takes the weekends off.

I navigate the stairwell as carefully as I can. Each step I take feels like someone's taking a jackhammer to my head, sending my brain ricocheting against the back of my skull. I can hardly see my feet on the stairs.

Thankfully, Marco appears a few feet in front of me and eyes me with concern. "You doing okay?" He jumps up the last few steps and puts my arm through his to support me the rest of the way down the stairwell. I can't remember a time he's done anything like this before.

When I reach the kitchen, there's already a plate of French toast and cut strawberries. The can of whipped cream sits beside a steaming cup of coffee. I don't have the heart to tell Marco I doubt I can stomach any of this. He obviously went through a lot of work. For a second, I wonder if Mom's paying him to be nice to me since I missed my senior trip. That would be one way to explain his unusual attentiveness.

"What's Dad doing home?" I ask as my brother sits beside me and digs into his own piled-up plate.

Marco shrugs. "Work. What else?"

We don't say anything for a few minutes while I pick at my food. Nobody in the family is as good a cook as Mom, but the French toast isn't bad. I'm pretty sure I'm hungry. If I could get past the nausea, I'd probably enjoy being spoiled like this by my big brother.

"After breakfast, you want to watch a movie?" Marco asks.

"Sure." I'd be up for a romcom, but I'm pretty sure Marco will want to pick something with action and superheroes. I just hope the explosions and fight scenes aren't too loud. I don't think my brain can handle that.

My stomach isn't so sure about the coffee, but my brain perks up after my first few sips. If I can make my way through the entire mug, maybe I'll be able to function. Marco has already finished his food and jumps up to clear the table.

"Take your time," he tells me, "and when you're ready, we'll get a movie started. Have you seen *Ant-Man and the Wasp* yet?"

"No," I answer. "Is it any good?"

CHAPTER 19

"So, what'd you think?" my brother asks when the movie's over.

"Aren't we supposed to wait for the part after the credits?" I ask.

Marco shrugs. "You can watch it, but you probably won't understand it unless you've seen the other movies." He turns off the TV. "What now? Think you're ready to join your class at the lake? Senior trip. That's a pretty big deal."

I hate the fact that all my friends are at my cabin with my mom having a great time without me, but I'm also sick enough that I know when to count my losses.

"I don't think I'm up for it," I tell my brother. "But thanks anyway."

He looks disappointed. Maybe Mom told him that if he nursed me back to health before my big weekend camping trip was over she'd give him an extra bonus. The worst part of the day is not being able to get in touch with anyone out there.

Marco said something earlier about Mom having to take my cell. I can't believe that in addition to missing out on my own senior trip, I can't even text my friends to find out what they're doing.

Then an idea strikes me. "Hey, do you have Chris's number in your phone?"

"Chris?" Marco feigns ignorance. "Who's Chris?"

"What do you mean who's Chris? My boyfriend."

"Oh. That Chris." Marco clears his throat. "No, I don't think so. Why?"

"I just wanted to see how he's doing." A nagging thought looms in the back of my head. "Hey, I know you have his number because you were the one he texted to figure out what I wanted for my birthday last year. Remember that?"

"Oh. Yeah. But I didn't save it or anything." He lets out a chuckle. "Truth be told, I didn't think you two'd be together that long."

I glare at him, and he shrugs. "Sorry."

"Could you at least check?" I ask.

Marco pulls out his phone, swipes at his screen a couple times, and announces, "Nope. Nothing from anyone named Chris."

I groan, and my brother aims the remote at the TV again. "Hey, since you're being such a good sport about all this, let's watch another movie. This time you pick. How about a romcom?"

We're halfway into *Thirteen Going on Thirty* when Dad comes into the living room. "Marco, can I talk to you?"

My brother leaves the movie going, but I hit pause once he leaves. My brain craves the silence, even if only for a few minutes.

"I've got the detective on the phone right now," Dad is hissing from the foyer. "He's on his way over to talk to Mia."

For a minute, I wonder if this is some fever-induced hallucination. I certainly feel sick enough to have made something like this up, but the concern in my brother's voice is unmistakable.

"What? He can't come over here. Not today."

Some sort of muffled exchange. I don't think I'd be able to follow their conversation if my life depended on it.

It feels strange hearing my Dad and Marco talking to each other at all. What's going on?

"... going to want to question her," Dad whispers.

"It'll be fine," Marco says. "I'll take care of everything." I don't know what to make of this new cooperative attitude between them.

"Like you did before?" Dad snaps. This is more like it. The

two of them always on edge with each other.

The strain of trying to listen in is too great. I make my way toward the stairs.

"Where are you going?" Marco calls to me a moment later.

"I need to lie down," I tell him.

A minute later I'm in bed, and he's handing me more water and another set of pills for my headache.

"What were you and Dad arguing about?" I ask. There's something that's not connecting in my brain. Maybe it's this headache. Maybe it's from being sick. I feel like I should understand more than I do. This whole day has felt like I'm listening to everything in a foreign language. I know the individual words but am slower piecing them together than I should be.

Marco gives a little chuckle. "Oh, nothing. Dad's just worried about work stuff. You know how he gets."

I take the pills and the cup of water my brother's holding out. "Thanks," I say. I had no idea that watching one and a half movies would make me so tired. I feel like I'm ready to sleep for the rest of the day and all through the night as well. So much for trying to get better in time to make it to my senior trip.

I hope they're all having a good time. When Mom comes back with my phone, I'll get to see all the pictures. In the meantime, I'm too sleepy to even care that I'm not there with my friends.

"Have a good nap," Marco tells me, pulling the blankets up to my chin as if I were a toddler. "Sleep as long as you'd like. Your body needs the rest."

CHAPTER 20

Springtime. I've always loved the …

What's that noise?

I glance at the clock. Half past four, except it's bright out. Bright as day.

I'm so confused.

My head hurts. Why does my head hurt? What time did I go to bed? I'm so tired …

I need to … Wait, what day is it? Half past four. Can't be nighttime. Not with the sky so bright. Not with …

What's that noise?

"Mia, I need you to get up. Now."

I don't understand. I think it must be … Someone's in my room. It's not Mom. What's going on?

"Mia, get up." It's my dad. But who's with him? Why are there strangers in my house?

"Are you dressed?" Dad asks. I think so. Am I? I have no idea what I'm doing here, why my head aches this badly.

Where's Mom?

"There are officers here," Dad says. Officers? Like cops? What do they want? "They have some questions for you," Dad tells me.

Questions? I've got questions. Is this about …

No. It can't be. I'm just confused. I might not even be awake at all. This whole thing must be one bad dream.

The police are here for me? Did Dad let them in? That can't mean that …

No, Dad would never allow that to happen. It must be something else.

I want my mom.

Dad steps in and pulls the covers off me. "Wake up," he says. "You're going with these guys."

Going? Where are we going? Where are they taking me? What's going on?

Dad squeezes my arm. Leans in. Acts as if he's going to kiss the top of my head, except he doesn't. His fingernails dig into my biceps. "Remember what I've taught you," he whispers, so quietly my brain might have made it up.

I glance at him questioningly, but he's too busy apologizing to the two officers. "She's pretty out of it."

Remember what I've taught you. So this is about …

"Miss Blanca, we have some questions we'd like to ask you," a man says. I don't think I've seen him before, but he acts as if he belongs here. There's no apologizing for waking me up in the middle of the night. Except it can't be night.

I'm still so confused.

Where's Mom? Is she the one who called the police here? Is she the one who told them …

I think I'm about to puke. There's something familiar about this fear. Something about this terror that triggers a latent memory, something that's been lost for a very, very long time.

I understand, or at least I think I do. I think I know what's going on. Why the police are here. What they want to ask me.

I look to Dad. *Remember what I've taught you.* He's got his arm around me. He's leading me out of my room. Down the hall and toward the stairs. His fingernails dig into my flesh. Is he as frightened as I am?

Remember what I've taught you.

What are the police going to ask me? I have to tell them the truth, don't I? Maybe not.

"It'll be okay," Dad says, and I seize onto his words. If Dad isn't worried, then I don't have any reason to be either. Dad knows how to handle things like this.

He always has.

That's why he's so good at what he does.

I'm outside now. The sun is bright, the pain in the back of my skull blasting me awake.

I'm passed from one set of hands to another. Led away to a waiting police car, like a criminal under arrest.

Dad remains on the porch, but his words are still with me.

His warning.

Remember what I've taught you.

A woman is sitting next to me. "Mia," she says. "Mia, do you know where you are?"

The question seems inane. "In a police car."

"Do you know what day today is?" Her voice is somber.

The day? Of course I remember … It's Friday. Senior skip day. No, that can't be right…

"Do you know what today is?" she repeats.

I stare at my father, standing motionless on our porch. I think about what I'm not supposed to tell the police, what I'm not supposed to tell anybody, then I shake my head.

The woman says something into a radio and buckles me in. "Come on. Let's go."

CHAPTER 21

This is about Dad. That's what this is. The police want to ask me questions about my father.

I was in middle school when I first started to understand. Started to put the pieces together. There was more to my dad, the man I loved, the man I idolized, than the loving family man I knew at home.

I was twelve or thirteen by the time I learned I had an older sister. Half-sister, I should say, from my dad's previous marriage. In the course of one overheard phone conversation, I discovered that when he was younger, my dad had been married and divorced, and that the half-sister I never knew I had had been murdered in a vicious attack.

I wasn't supposed to know any of this, and so I kept my mouth shut, but I wondered if that had something to do with the creepy men Dad called over for late-night business meetings when everyone else in the house was supposed to be asleep.

Another time I overheard Dad fighting with my brother.

Marco threatening to call the police on him. "You do that," Dad snarled, "and the same thing'll happen to you." I didn't know who or what he was referring to, but something in the way he said it made me realize it was more than an idle threat.

That's when Marco left home. Stopped talking with Dad altogether.

Looking back, maybe I should have been more concerned than I was. But when you're young and you hear your adult brother and your father fighting, making threats, you don't stop to think that something dangerous might be going on. It's grown-up stuff. Between Dad and Marco.

And then I got even older. Started to realize my dad had made more enemies than friends in the business world, and the friends he did have scared me. More than once, I was woken up in the middle of the night by voices outside, Dad talking to some stranger in the shadows. I could never hear what they were saying and knew better than to try to listen.

When I was in tenth grade, the police started coming by. Asking Mom questions. Sometimes Dad would come home complaining about cops tailing him around all day. He was a busy man. An important man. They didn't understand the line of work he was in.

The truth was that I didn't understand the line of work he

was in either.

"Some things we keep in the family," Dad would tell me. "Some things we keep to ourselves." That part I understood. Understood without understanding, if something like that's even possible. It wasn't my job to get too curious. I took my cues from Mom. Didn't ask questions. Accepted life as it was. Knew my father loved me more than anything, and that was enough for me.

When Dad's phone beeped at dinnertime and the color drained from his face and we didn't see him for weeks, I didn't ask where he was. Didn't mention he was gone. And then he'd come home, smothering Mom and me with gifts, and everything went back to normal again.

Remember what I've taught you. What did Dad mean when he said that? I have no idea what he's afraid of, what information I might give the police that could or couldn't get him in trouble. I've never been scared of my father, not a single moment in my life. Dad's never raised his voice to me or Mom. Not ever. I told myself for years that whatever was going on with work was his business. Adult stuff. Things I couldn't understand.

But the truth is I understood more than I gave myself credit for. Understood that some things weren't supposed to be discussed with outsiders. Some things were supposed to stay within the family.

I have no idea why the police decided to start tailing my dad two years ago. I have no idea what they think I do or don't know now or why they want to question me. But I'm scared.

Scared that some way, somehow, I might say something that will get my dad in trouble. Because even though I don't get exactly who he is in the business world, I know that he loves me. And I love him.

Remember what I've taught you.

How am I supposed to remember what I never knew to begin with?

My legs are trembling. I feel disoriented. A little dizzy. Is it just nerves? I still don't remember falling asleep in the middle of the day. The mental confusion certainly isn't helping my anxiety.

I think about Sandy, the woman who led the teen girls' Bible study I was in for a while. Even though she had a lot going on in her own life, she was always a picture of perfect calm. Peace just seemed to radiate from her. I'm not as spiritual as she is, but I could definitely use some of that peace right now.

The only problem is I don't know how to find it. I always assumed that once I got older, I'd learn to be more like Sandy. I quit the teen Bible study because I was busy with school. Story of my life. Focus on my grades, get my NYU scholarship. Then I would start thinking more about things like God and religion.

Except now I'm in the back of a police car. I don't know what they're going to ask me, but I'm terrified about what might happen before this mess is resolved. I want to pray. Sandy always acts as if it's not hard at all. You just open your mouth and talk to God. But it comes so easily to her. She could pray for hours at a time if she wanted. I've never done much more than the kind of praying you do before Thanksgiving dinner. But I really need God's help now.

I sure hope he's listening.

I shoot up a plea to heaven. I have no idea if I use the right phrases. I have no idea if it's going to make any difference whatsoever. And I certainly don't feel the peace that Sandy always talked about. But I have to believe that I did the right thing anyway. Prayer is about the only thing I know to do right now.

I wish I had my phone on me. I need to text Chris. Call my mom. Let everyone know what's happening to me. Dad knows just about every lawyer in the city. He could tell me what to do. He could help me figure all this out.

But Dad's not here. Mom's not here. Chris's not here. And I don't have my phone.

What's that verse Sandy always quotes? *God works all*

things out for good. Something like that. It's one of Chris's favorites too. I know he uses it when things are going hard for him at home.

God works all things out for good. Which means that I just need to get through this scary part and then everything will be fine. What was that story of the police who barged into the wrong home and then got sued and they owed the family hundreds of thousands of dollars for damages or something like that? I don't remember the details now, but what if this is something like that? I just need to have faith. Need to trust that what Sandy and Chris believe is really true.

God's going to make good things happen because of what's going on right now. I need to be patient. The police are going to realize they've made a mistake, and we'll get everything fixed and sorted out.

Patience has never been a virtue of mine. What's that joke Christians always say? Don't pray for patience or God will give it to you. Maybe that's what this is. Some big test. Every once in a while, I feel like Chris wishes I took my faith as seriously as he does. Is this God's way of answering my boyfriend's prayer?

I'm about to find out.

I've never been to the police station before. I never even

realized until now that it was this close to our house. This won't take long. I know it won't. Dad's probably on the phone now, making sure I get out of here as soon as possible.

We pull up to the curb, and the officer lets me out of the back seat. I tell myself she's just doing her job. Trying to be helpful. That if I smile and act compliant and polite, she'll realize I'm not a threat and send me back home to my family. Where I need to be.

The officer doesn't return my smile, and I'm not sure what to make of that. In fact, I think I can safely say that she's frowning at me. Then she opens her mouth, and the first words I hear are, "All right, Mia. We have a lot to talk about. Starting with what you know about how your mother and boyfriend both ended up dead."

CHAPTER 22

"Where's your mom going?" Chris asks when I let him in the back door of the cabin.

"Has some errands to run," I tell him. If he didn't look so serious, I'd make some kind of joke about how she could come back any minute so he better not try to get too close or anything.

But he's staring at me so intently. I have no idea what's on his mind or what he's about to say.

"Come on." He brushes past me into the living room. I follow him toward the largest couch, and my stomach drops when he says, "We have to talk."

I try not to let him see my panic. Try not to show him how scared I am. If he's planning on breaking up with me, couldn't he at least do it at the end of the weekend? Let me enjoy just a couple more happy days with my friends?

I force a smile. Tell myself I'm being ridiculous. Chris and I are destined to be together. I'm the only one who knows his family secrets. I'm the only one he trusts. Not to mention the

100

fact that we're in love. We're meant to be together.

Chris is fidgeting in his seat. "Listen, Mia."

"Hold on," I interrupt. I can't help it. If Chris wants to break up with me, he has every right to in the world. Just not now. Not here. Not like this. "Maybe we should go back out to the dock. It's such a nice day. And ... and ..." I feel my voice rising. This is no good. I can't get all irrational right now. I have to think clearly.

Clearly.

Just listen to what he has to say, I tell myself. It's an order. I shut my lips.

"Mia, I think you're an amazing girl," he begins, and that's when I know. This is it. This is goodbye. This is the end.

I'm off the couch. "I need some fresh air," I say. "Let's go out." I'm not thinking about Mom's silly water safety rules, which made tons of sense when I was a preschooler but now are just fueled by paranoia. Dad checks the wood on the dock every single year, and besides, I've been swimming since I could walk.

My palms are sweaty when Chris and I reach the water's edge. He doesn't argue when I leave the cabin, just follows me out here. Well, at least if he's going to dump me, it won't be in front of twenty of our classmates. Got to give him props for that much at least.

I don't want to do this. Don't want to go through it. No sense of timing. None whatsoever.

I cross my arms and face him. The sun's behind his shoulder, blinding me, but I don't care. I squint, which probably makes me look more intimidating than scared. Good.

"So," I say, jutting out my hip as defiantly as I can, "what is it you want to tell me?"

Chris is staring at his feet. This is one time when I wish he wasn't so soft-spoken, wish he wasn't so polite. After you've been with someone for three full years, after you've grown as close as we have, there's no such thing as a gentle breakup. He needs to just say it and get this torturous silence over with.

Chris swallows so hard I can hear his throat working. For a minute, I suspect he's waiting for me to be the next to talk, but he's dead wrong if he thinks I'm about to make this easy on him.

I brace myself. Remind myself that uncertainty is always worse than the truth. Haven't I been terrified for weeks that Chris and I would break up? At least now I'll know where I stand.

I can handle this. I can be mature. I can be an adult.

I hold my breath.

Chis fidgets with his hands. "I had a dream last night," he

tells me. "A dream from God."

I squint even harder. "What did you just say?"

"A dream from God. Look," he rushes on, "I know it sounds kind of crazy, and I know sometimes dreams are just dreams, but this one was different. Just hear me out, okay?"

"Okay."

He sits down on the dock, dangling his feet in the water. I feel silly standing here with my arms crossed, so I do the same.

"I think God wants me to become a pastor."

It's not what I was expecting to hear, but I try not to show my surprise. I can tell that Chris is in one of those pensive moods he gets, and I know from experience it's best to let him talk it all out.

At least he's not breaking up with me. Not yet.

"I can't explain it," he begins, and I can sense the confidence rising in his tone, "but in my dream, I was there in front of a church telling hundreds of people about Jesus. It was the most intense feeling I've ever experienced."

I swallow down my jealousy. I thought his love for me would be the most intense feeling he's experienced. I don't tell him this. Instead I keep listening. His voice only grows in excitement.

"And I was just ... the Bible verses, they were just coming out of my mouth. You know I've never been all that good of a speaker, and I don't even like to talk when the teacher calls on me in class. But I wasn't scared or nervous or anything. I was just … I was there in front of the church, and people were listening to me, and it was like … It was like God was right there. Talking through me. I don't even know what I was saying. My only thought was it must be God speaking through me because that was the only way to describe it. It was amazing."

"Wow." I literally don't have anything else to say.

Fortunately, Chris is ready to keep on talking. "So I woke up, and it was the middle of the night, and I was praying and praying and praying, and I told God that if he was calling me to become a pastor, then yes I was going to become a pastor."

He hesitates for a minute, and that's when I realize what this discussion is all about. It's not about me or our relationship at all. It's about something that hits much closer to home for Chris.

Much closer.

"What about your dad?" I ask quietly.

"Well, that's the thing," he answers. "For the first time, I didn't feel scared. I didn't feel worried. In fact, I wrote him a letter last night and left it for him."

"What'd you say?" I want to be excited for Chris. I really

do. I want to be excited and supportive and encouraging and everything else a good girlfriend should be. But I know about Chris's dad. I know better than just about anyone. And all I feel is dread.

"I told him that God gave me a sign that he wants me to become a pastor. And if that means my dad wants to disown me, I'm willing to take up my cross and bear that burden."

"What about Gabriella?" This doesn't make sense. Chris wouldn't do anything to risk his sister's safety.

"She's with her grandma all week, so it's perfect timing. I think that's why God waited to give me that dream until last night. Because I can do something now. I can make a difference."

"I don't know if that's such a good idea," I whisper. I'm not scared about Chris breaking up with me anymore. I'm scared for an entirely different reason.

Chris shrugs. "That's probably what I would have said a week ago, but if you would have just seen that dream. If you could have just ..." He's leaning toward me. Looking right at me. Begging me to understand. "It was so real," he tries again. "And if this is what God wants me to do, if this is what he's calling me to ..."

I want to hold him. To hug him and protect him and show him that nothing in the world means more to me than his happiness. And I know God makes him happy. I really do. And I know that if he had the chance, Chris would make an amazing pastor. He's so kind and encouraging, and he loves God with all his heart. But he's not thinking things through right now. He's on one of those spiritual highs, like when you go to a camp or retreat or something and get all fired up for Christ, but then you come home and that excitement dwindles down.

That's what this is. A flash. A spark. This isn't sustainable. Not for someone like Chris. Not with a dad like his.

I have to reason with him. Have to make him understand.

He grabs my hand, and there's an intensity burning in his eyes I've never seen before. I want to believe this dream really was a message from God. I desperately want to believe it. But I know Mr. Gomez. And I know what he'll do when he reads that letter.

The letter.

My stomach flops. "Where's that note you wrote him?" I demand. "What'd you do with it?"

"I left it on the dashboard of his truck so he'll see it when he leaves for work this morning."

What time is it? I have to think. Chris's dad starts work before lunch. That means … Oh, no. He's already seen it. He's already read it.

Chris kisses the top of my head. "I want you to be happy for me," he whispers.

"I'm happy for you," I lie, while inwardly I'm trying to think of anybody I could call to run interference for us. Maybe his dad's so hungover today he'll be late for work. Maybe there's someone I could ask to swing by Chris's house ... His truck might be unlocked. If I can get a hold of my brother, I can ask him to do it. Pull up in Chris's driveway, find a way to get into that truck, and grab the letter. Make sure his dad never sees it.

Ever.

"There's something else," Chris says.

My throat clenches because now I know what he's going to do. And I know that neither of us is ready for this. Not really. As much as we love each other, as good a fit as we are together, this isn't the right time.

Chris is on his knee. He's holding out a jewelry box.

"I know it won't be easy being married to a pastor," he's saying, and I have to clench my jaw shut to keep my sob contained. "I can't promise we'll earn as much money as you're used to, but there's something else about the dream I haven't told you yet. You were in it too. We had ..." His voice cracks with emotion. "We had a church of our own. A little country church. And you were there, and I was there, and you were sitting in the front row, and you were so proud of me, and ..."

He sniffs. "Mia, will you marry me? Will you be my wife?"

I crumple to the ground beside him. We have to figure this out. We don't have much time.

Chris wipes away my tear with his thumb, looks at me with a sheepish grin, and says, "Well?"

He probably thinks I'm crying because I'm so happy. Everything makes sense now. The conversation with Mom, Chris calling my dad at work ...

I support you a hundred percent. That's what Mom said. *Whatever decisions you make for your future, I support you a hundred percent.*

I kiss Chris on the corner of his mouth. I want him to know how much I love him. How much I adore him. And that yes, one day I want to be his wife.

One day ...

This wasn't what was supposed to happen. This whole weekend ...

"Say something," Chris pleads.

I open my mouth and choke on a sob.

Chris slips the ring box back into his pocket. "Are you not ready? Should we wait?"

He's worried that I'm upset about the proposal. He really

has no idea, does he?

"Chris." I can barely say his name without suffocating with emotion.

"I should have waited, shouldn't I? We're too young. Is that it? A promise ring. Would that have been better?"

I shake my head. It doesn't matter what he chooses to call it. Engagement ring. Promise ring. Wedding ring.

Because there are two things I know in the bottom of my soul to be true.

That Chris and I are meant to be together.

And that his father will never let him become a pastor.

"Tell me what you're thinking," Chris says. "I want to know how you feel."

"I'm scared," I admit to his shoulder, clinging with all my might to the back of his shirt. The truth is I've never been this afraid in my life.

"Why are you scared?" he asks.

"Because when your dad gets that letter," I answer, "he's going to kill you."

CHAPTER 23

"Mia?" the policewoman says. "Did you hear me? Do you understand what I've just told you?"

I stare at the metal desk inside the police station, hardly able to focus on her words.

"What can you tell me about how your mother and boyfriend died?"

"They aren't dead," I tell her. Shouldn't that be enough to clear up the mistake? "I want to talk to my mom."

The woman's expression doesn't change. I feel my throat closing. I can't let panic take over. Not now. Not here. I have to sort this out.

"Text Chris," I tell her. "He'll explain everything. I can't … I don't remember. Just call him. I want to talk to my mom."

"Mia, do you know what day it is?" She keeps harping on the stupid date. It could be February 31 for all I care. That doesn't explain why I'm in a police station with a woman who's insisting the two people I love the most in the world have died.

"It's Friday," I tell her. It's senior skip weekend. I'm supposed to be at the cabin. I feel like I'm going to throw up. When the police picked me up, I thought it must be about Dad. What else could it have been?

Remember what I've taught you. That's what he told me before the police put me in their car. I thought the woman brought me here to ask about Dad's work. Instead, she's sitting here telling me that Mom and Chris are dead. It's absurd. Doesn't make any sense.

Dead. The word replays and replays in my head like a choppy gif. *Dead. Dead. Dead.*

Your mother and boyfriend are dead.

They can't be dead. We still have to go to the cabin.

But I didn't make it to the cabin. Instead I got sick …

My brother was here. He was taking care of me. Or maybe that's just what I was dreaming. How did I wake up in the middle of the afternoon unable to remember anything?

I was watching a movie. A movie with my brother. We were watching that one … Dancing. It had dancing in it. No, that must have been part of the dream too.

This woman keeps asking me what day it is, but all I can hear is one taunting word.

Dead.

Dead. Dead. Dead.

She can't really mean that. It's a mistake. She thinks I'm someone else, except she's calling me Mia.

What is going on?

Your mother and boyfriend are dead.

It's so ridiculous I'd be laughing my head off if I weren't so scared. But these cops don't joke. They don't mess around. This isn't some kind of juvenile senior-weekend prank.

Your mother and boyfriend are dead.

I try to wrap my mind around the concept, wondering curiously at how the words seem both so strange and yet somewhat familiar. Like I've had this exact same dream before, been in this exact same room, carried on this exact same conversation with this exact same officer. But I know I haven't.

"Now listen, Mia." The officer's talking to me like I'm an infant. "I need you to fill this out and sign it. Then our detective will be in to speak with you shortly."

I manage to keep myself as composed as can be expected. My hand shakes while I fill out her paperwork, a trembling that doesn't subside even after she leaves me here in this room alone. Every time I hear footsteps in the hallway, I imagine it's Mom come to rescue me and clear up this entire mistake.

But they're telling me Mom's dead. She can't be, though. We had plans …

And Chris … We were going to go to the cabin. It was our class trip. I need to think straight. Need to remember …

I don't know how long they've kept me waiting here in this claustrophobic room. I'm afraid I'm going to suffocate when the door opens. In comes a tall man with a Styrofoam cup in his hand and a scowl etched onto his face. "You remember me?"

I shake my head. Am I supposed to know who he is?

He sets his cup on the table and sits down across from me. "Detective Drisklay. We've met before."

I want to tell him that he's mistaken, that I've never seen him in my life, but something stops me. Another flash of *deja vu*. Was this man in my dreams too?

"You sure you don't know me?"

I stare again. The flash is gone. I shake my head.

He doesn't seem surprised or disappointed at my admission. Instead, he pulls out an electronic device and tells me we'll be recording.

"You understand your rights?" is one of the first questions he asks.

I nod. "I think so."

"I need a yes or no answer, Miss Blanca," he states dryly.

I swallow. "Yes."

Drisklay leans forward. "What can you tell me about the events at your parents' cabin the afternoon of May 24?"

113

I pause. "I haven't been at the cabin. I was supposed to go, but …"

He stares at me then lets out a frustrated sigh. "Miss Blanca, have you met with the mental health liaison yet?"

"The who?"

"Our mental health liaison. She was supposed to fill you in. Is it possible you met with her and have forgotten?"

I shake my head. "I've been here alone waiting this whole time," I tell him.

"One minute." Drisklay turns off the recorder then stands up, his chair making a terrible scraping sound against the concrete floor, and he leaves the room

I'm cold. I'm scared. I'm confused. And I need to talk to my mother.

Drisklay comes back in a moment later. Sits down. Turns his device back on. "Miss Blanca, unfortunately our liaison is unable to join us for the time being. The abbreviated version is you've suffered a brain injury. Your short-term memory has been impaired, making it hard for you to create any new memories or remember events for the past three months."

Three months? I can't have heard him right.

He takes a sip of coffee and levels his eyes at me. "Do you understand?"

What am I supposed to say? Of course I don't understand. "Not really," I admit.

His annoyance is palpable when he lets out his breath. "Today is August 14. Three months ago, you were at the cabin with your mother and Christopher Gomez. You survived an assault. Your mother was killed. Initially, we believed Gomez to be the attacker."

"He would never do that," I interject.

Drisklay doesn't appear to hear me, or if he does hear me, he doesn't care. "Just this morning," he goes on without pause, "we found Gomez's body in the lake by your parents' property. So now we have two murder victims, and we have you."

"I don't know anything." The room spins, and I'm trying hard to keep myself from falling. I grab onto the sides of my chair until my forearms hurt from the strain. "I don't know what you're talking about."

"What's the last thing you remember?" he asks.

"I woke up from a nap. The police were in my room. My dad said they had questions for me."

Drisklay keeps his voice steady and even. "Right now, I need you to focus on the facts of May 24."

"I'm telling you, I don't know. I thought that was today. I honestly ..." I stop. Did he say it's already August? "I don't remember anything." It's become like my own personal slogan.

115

My go-to response for everything.

"Then let's talk about today," Drisklay says. "Before you went to take your nap, what were you doing?"

That's easy. I was ... I was ... I'm so frustrated I want to cry, but my need for answers takes precedence over my need for some kind of emotional release.

"Who was at home with you when you went to bed?" Drisklay asks.

"My mom and my ..." I stop. That can't be right. The detective's telling me my mom is dead, that she died three whole months ago. Do I believe him? It has to be some sort of mistake, doesn't it?

He lets out his breath in a forced huff. "Miss Blanca, I'm sure that this is all something of a shock to you, but we have reason to believe that your mother and your boyfriend were both killed by the same perp, who also assaulted you and may have reason to cause you harm."

"He's after me now?"

"That's why we brought you into police custody," Drisklay says. "For your protection."

"But I thought ..." I pause, trying to remember everything that happened from the moment I woke up. "They said that ..." I look around at the interrogation room, realizing this meeting has nothing to do with my father. Confusion morphs to relief, relief that lasts for all of a second. Then full realization of everything else sweeps over me. My mother is dead. And Chris.

This isn't some sort of mistake then. It's true. It really happened.

And I don't remember a single thing.

CHAPTER 24

"I'm sorry," Sandy says as she rushes through the door of the police room. "I came as quickly as I could, but traffic was something awful." She sweeps by the officer holding open the door and nearly trips on the carpet. I'm out of the cement room at least. The mental health liaison I finally met said I shouldn't have ever been set up in the interrogation rooms in the first place, explaining that I have to forgive Detective Drisklay, who sometimes forgets the difference between victims and suspects.

I'm not ashamed to confess that I had a complete breakdown while the detective was questioning me. As soon as I realized this meeting wasn't about my dad, I stopped focusing on my own survival and understood that everything the police were telling me was true. Mom is gone. So is Chris. Killed.

By the same person who attacked me and left me with nothing but long-term memories.

Drisklay couldn't handle my tears or decipher my sobs, so he pulled the liaison out of whatever it was that she was doing.

She was the one who moved us to this more comfortable room and asked if there was anybody I could call. I thought about my dad but decided on Sandy and gave the woman the name of our church.

Now Sandy's here, smothering me in hugs and tears. "I'm so sorry you're going through this, sweetie. I can't even begin to guess how hard this must be for you."

I've told the liaison about my headache. She's going to pull up my medical files to see if I'm on any pain killers. Until then, she tells me to take three Tylenol. It seems like a lot to me, but I'm not going to argue.

Sandy's been fretting over me and praying over me since she came in. I think Drisklay and the liaison know it's time to back off a little on the questioning.

Once I stop crying, I'm able to put my thoughts into some sort of logical order, or at least I try to. Mom is dead. Not only dead but murdered. The police haven't given me any more information than that, so I have no idea if she was shot, if she was strangled, drowned. Maybe she was stabbed and left in that cabin to bleed out, terrified and alone ...

Then they tell me Chris was a suspect at one point, which is absolutely ridiculous, but I can't be upset about that because now it's come out that he's one of the victims. Found in the lake just this morning. The lake by our cabin ...

But that's not all. I've also learned in the past twenty minutes that I've been the victim of a terrible assault that's robbed me of any ability to form short-term memories. Sandy tells me that every morning I wake up and imagine it's senior skip day all over again. Like that Adam Sandler movie, except there's absolutely nothing funny about my situation. Nothing funny at all.

I have all my memories from before the attack, but Drisklay needs answers about what happened that day. Everyone assumes I was an eyewitness to the crime and that I should be able to give them a name to find justice for the ones I've lost.

Except my mind is a complete blank. It's not as if I have a vague memory of that day but just run into difficulties pulling up details. It's as if that day never happened at all. I'm so confused, and I know Sandy's trying to help, but she's fretting over me so much now I feel like I'll suffocate.

"The doctors thought you'd recover in a week or two at most," she's telling me. "It's been so hard for your family."

"I want to go home," I state, but Drisklay shakes his head.

"Not possible," he states flatly.

"What about with me?" Sandy asks. "What if I took her to my home for the night? She needs sleep. All this stress can't be good for her."

Drisklay frowns as if considering. "If she saw the perp and could give us an ID …"

"I keep telling you I don't remember anything."

Sandy gives me another squeeze.

"I believe you." It's possibly the very first thing Drisklay's said to me all evening that makes me even think he might be on my side. "But it doesn't matter what I think. If the culprit assumes you have information …" He doesn't finish his thought. I imagine that I should be able to connect the dots myself, but I'm so tired and my head hurts too much.

I'm thankful when Sandy finishes for him. "You think Mia could be in danger?"

"It's a possibility."

"But she's been safe these past few months, right?" Sandy asks positively.

Drisklay shrugs. "That was when Gomez was our suspect."

"Oh." Sandy looks at me. "Well, she needs to sleep somewhere. And as far as I can tell, my place is as safe as any."

He shakes his head. "Can't do that."

Sandy straightens her back. "And why not?"

"Because if she goes to sleep now, she wakes up in the morning and we have to go over this entire ordeal all over again."

I blink, finally understanding. Is this what it means to suffer the degree of short-term memory loss that I have? That every day I'm destined to wake up and have to learn all over again that the people I love are dead? And that somewhere out there is a man who tried to kill me once and may return at any point to finish the job?

"But you can't keep her awake forever," Sandy protests.

"It's okay," I interrupt.

She turns to look at me as if she'd forgotten I possess the capacity for human speech.

"It's okay," I repeat. "I can stay awake. Maybe it'll ..." I glance at Drisklay. "Maybe it'll help me remember."

Now Sandy's the one frowning, and the detective's scowl looks one shade less grumpy.

"What about photos?" I ask. "Something that might help trigger the memories? Do you think something like that might work?"

Drisklay tosses his Styrofoam cup into the trash and studies me. I can't tell from his expression if he's surprised, impressed, or plotting my execution.

"Are you sure, honey?" Sandy whispers. "This has been a stressful day ..."

"And tomorrow's going to be just as stressful," I remind her. The thought of waking up every single morning only to rediscover the shock that it's not my senior class trip, that my mother and boyfriend are dead ... I can't handle that. I have to help the detective as much as I can tonight.

"But eventually you'll need to sleep," Sandy persists, so I tell her when I'm tired, I'll take a break.

"Right now," I conclude decisively, "all I need to do is help the detective solve this case. Which means I need to remember everything."

CHAPTER 25

"How are you doing?" Sandy asks. It's sweet that she's still here. That she's so concerned about me. It's getting late. She has her own family to take care of, but she hasn't left my side.

"I could use some more Tylenol," I say.

While she goes out to find me some pain pills, Drisklay lays photographs on the desk in front of me. "This is where we found your mom," he says, pointing to a picture of the living room of our cabin. It's been a couple hours already, and I have no idea how long it will be until my memory resets again.

I rehearse everything in my head, from the most basic — Mom and Chris are dead — to the crime scene details Drisklay's described. It was my best friend Kelsie who found Mom inside the cabin. Knife wounds. Blunt force trauma. Drisklay hasn't shown me the pictures of her body, thank God. It's hard enough looking at the blood stains on the cabin floor. Kelsie's boyfriend was there too. Performed CPR.

If only he could have saved her.

When and how Chris was killed is still anybody's guess. Up until his body was discovered by fishermen this morning, police assumed he was the culprit.

How are you supposed to react when you learn both your mom and your boyfriend have been killed? Whenever I think about Chris, I feel terrible that I'm not grieving for Mom. Sandy says that sometimes you need to mourn in procession. First for one. Then for the other.

It's not a journey I'm looking forward to embarking on.

Which is part of the reason why I'm so intent on staying awake. On helping Drisklay find my attacker, no matter what it takes. I have no idea how long my memory of today will last, but I do know from what Sandy and Drisklay both have said that if I fall asleep, it'll be a total reset. Like shutting down your computer when you've forgotten to save your documents. Except in my case, there's no cloud storage backing it all up. Or if there is, I have no idea how to access it.

"Can you tell me about your relationship with Gomez?" Drisklay asks. He's been surprisingly polite ever since I refused to leave and spend the night at Sandy's.

It feels weird talking to this middle-aged man about my boyfriend. What does he want to know? I tell him that we were in a few of the same classes at school, how we got closer once he started coming to youth group. I tell the detective about

Chris's father. I think that must be important, but apparently Drisklay knows Mr. Gomez even better than I do and doesn't need me to fill in any of those details.

"Have you talked with his dad?" I ask Drisklay.

"He's certainly kept our interest throughout this investigation," is his cryptic response.

Sandy comes back. Hands me three more pills. "You sure you should take that many?" she asks.

No, I'm not sure, but it's the only chance I have to keep my brain even halfway alert. Tylenol, coffee, and chips from the vending machine down the hall. Sandy tells me one of my symptoms from my injuries is nausea, but so far, I'm doing okay in that respect.

She stays on one side of the room, dozing every so often in an oversized chair while Drisklay hands me photograph after photograph. One thing he wants me to do is look at everything in the cabin, find out if anything might be missing. It looks just like our cabin always has, except of course for the blood stains on the floor, the broken glass, the overturned coffee table.

"Is this jogging any memories whatsoever?" Drisklay asks.

"No." I wish I had another answer to give. I've taken AP psychology. I know how the brain works. The memories have to still be there somewhere, right? I just need to access them.

I yawn and stretch. The physical movement makes me realize I'm still hungry. "I'm going to the vending machine."

Drisklay doesn't argue.

I slip by Sandy, who's sleeping with her head resting on her shoulder so she looks like a human-sized mother bird. I check to see how much change I have in my pocket from the ten-dollar bill she loaned me earlier. I'm trying to decide if I feel like a granola bar or some trail mix when I hear a loud grunt.

"Look. It's the spoiled little rich girl who got me into this mess in the first place."

I snap my head up, trying to remember where I've seen this man before.

He spits in my direction while two officers struggle to hurry him past. "Yeah, I know you. Filling my boy's head with your religious trash ..."

Drisklay appears in the hall the moment I realize I'm staring at Chris's father. The detective yells at the officers, telling them to keep their man away from his station, then turns to me.

"Come on," he says gruffly. "Next time you want a snack, you tell me what to get. No more wandering the hallways alone."

I feel like a guilty dog who's been caught rummaging through the trash, and I follow Drisklay with my head bowed. Seeing Chris's dad reminds me how real this case is. How real and how dangerous.

"Are they arresting him?" I ask once we're back at Drisklay's desk.

"All he's here for is to answer some questions."

I wonder how common it is to bring an innocent person in for questioning at this time of night, but Drisklay doesn't seem to be in a very talkative mood. Seeing Mr. Gomez has reminded me of something.

Something I think I should have remembered. Something I think must be important.

"Chris hates his dad," I tell Drisklay.

"I know," is all he answers.

"He's really mean. Like, abusive and stuff."

Drisklay nods. "I know."

Well, if he knows all that, I want to ask him why he hasn't arrested Mr. Gomez already, but I'm still busy trying to pinpoint what it is I'm supposed to recall.

Think, Mia. Think.

All of our talking has woken Sandy up. She comes over, giving my back a gentle rub. "You've had a long night, huh?" she says. "You sure you don't want to get some rest? You could even nap right here. That office chair isn't half bad if you're in need of a snooze."

I shake my head. I can't sleep. Can't afford to lose everything I've learned yet again. I really should start writing notes to myself so when I do forget, I won't have to waste time getting reminded. But writing notes would mean slowing down right now, and I'm so close to figuring it out. I know that I am. I just need a little more time ...

"Chris wrote his dad a letter," I announce, feeling both proud of myself for retrieving this lost piece of information and hopeful that it will give Drisklay the missing piece he needs to solve this case and put Chris's dad away for good.

"A letter," I repeat. Saying the words brings the rest of the memories rushing back. "Chris wanted to become a pastor. He told his dad before we drove out to the cabin. And I was worried because I knew his dad would be angry ..."

"Mr. Gomez has an alibi." Drisklay doesn't even look up from the file he's perusing.

"What?"

"An alibi. It wasn't him. We've got a dozen witnesses who place him at work that afternoon, and the place's got him on their security camera too. It wasn't Gomez."

"But he could have sent somebody," I say, feeling more uncertain with each word. "If he was angry enough, he might have ..." I let my voice trail off when I see the incredulity in Drisklay's face. Half the time, Chris's dad is too drunk to buy more beer, let alone hire someone to stage such an elaborate and violent assault.

If Chris's father wasn't the attacker, I need to remember something else. It's turning into a very long night, but as heavy as my eyelids are, I can't let myself sleep.

"Can I have another cup of coffee?" I ask the detective, remembering how upset he got at me for going to the vending machine on my own. It's not until Drisklay leaves that I realize I still haven't had anything else to eat, either.

Sandy gives me a reassuring hug. "You're doing great, sweetie. I'm so proud of you."

"You really don't have to stay here," I tell her. "I know it's getting late."

She frowns and cocks her head to the side like she's studying me for a test. "I don't mind."

I think about Sandy's family, about her husband and son. "You should go on home and get some rest."

It takes several more times to assure Sandy that I really will be okay without her, and she agrees to go.

"Was that the pastor's wife taking off?" Drisklay asks when he returns, handing me a mug of coffee as well as a store-bought Danish.

"Yeah. It's getting late." For a second, I think about asking

Drisklay if he needs to go home soon too, but then I change my mind.

The coffee is hot and strong. There's no sweetener, so I alternate between bites of the oversweet Danish and sips of the black coffee. Soon my thinking clears, and my headache eases up a little more.

Sugar and caffeine. God's wonder drugs.

Drisklay pulls out the stool he's been sitting on all night. "All right," he says. "Let's see what else you can remember."

CHAPTER 26

It's past midnight when Drisklay informs me that Chris's dad has been questioned and released. And even though he didn't act like the typical parent whose son has been found drowned in a lake, there's no reason to suspect that Mr. Gomez had anything to do with the attacks.

"We've asked him multiple times about the letter his son wrote," Drisklay tells me. "Gomez maintains that his son is a fool for wanting to enter into the ministry, but he wouldn't have bothered going after him. That and the fact that surveillance footage, witness testimony, as well as the GPS in Gomez's phone and truck all place him at work the afternoon of the attack. He's not our guy."

I hear Drisklay's words, understand their inherent logic, but still have a hard time letting go of Mr. Gomez as the prime suspect. Because if he didn't kill Mom and Chris, who did?

And even more baffling, why?

Drisklay and the other investigators have already ruled out

some kind of burglary gone wrong for about as many reasons as anyone would care to rattle off. Nothing important was stolen from the cabin. The crime took place in broad daylight. And the severity and nature of the injuries suggest a fit of rage as opposed to a botched attempt to steal some valuables.

Drisklay wants me to stop thinking about the crime scene and go farther back. People who might have been angry at my father and want to take it out on his family. I know Dad has plenty of enemies, but I have no idea who they are. Drisklay even asks about any PTA parents my mom might have ticked off. I laugh when he suggests this before I realize he's serious.

No. Nobody on the PTA would have wanted to kill my mom. Besides, why would they go after me and Chris, too?

Drisklay gives me far too many details about Chris's discovery. "Unfortunately, because of the degree of decomposition, we can't determine Gomez's direct time of death."

I wish Drisklay would stop talking about my boyfriend like this, but I suppose he's got to stay somewhat clinical to keep on doing the work he does day in and day out.

"Because we don't know exactly when he died," Drisklay continues, "we can't recreate the line of events. Did the attacker come after you and then Gomez tried to stop him?"

Yes, that sounds exactly like what Chris would do.

"The fact is," Drisklay says before I can respond, "we simply don't know. For now, let's just assume that Chris was an unfortunate bystander and that whoever came to your cabin was after you or your mom."

I'm trying to follow his line of reasoning, but I've grown so tired the room has started to spin. I've got the sense that I'm rocking slightly back and forth, but that could also be my vision blurring in and out of focus.

"Think," Drisklay tells me. "Who might have reason to attack you? Why would anybody want to do that?"

The truth? My mom was the kindest, most generous woman in the entire world. And I'm not really the sort of girl to walk around school making enemies either, much less enemies who get so upset they go on a killing spree.

"I really don't know," I answer. I'm frustrated. Frustrated with the investigation, frustrated with myself. If it weren't for this stupid brain injury, I could remember everything. Tell Drisklay exactly what he needs to know and get whoever did this behind bars.

It's infuriating. I need to remember, but it's not coming to me fast enough. In fact, it's not coming to me at all. It's been hours since I recalled what I did about Chris's letter to his dad, and as it turns out, Drisklay had known about Chris's note already.

I've got to press on. Got to try harder.

But I'm so tired.

"Hey." It's not until Drisklay snaps his fingers in front of my face that I realize I'm drifting off. Even after my second mug of coffee.

"Sorry." I jerk myself alert, but a few seconds later I'm swaying in my seat again.

"Go." Drisklay points to the oversized chair.

I can scarcely hear him, let alone understand what his gesture is supposed to mean. "Huh?"

"Go." He points again. "Sleep. You obviously can't function anymore." He says the words like it's something to be ashamed of, but I'm not going to let him dismiss me so easily.

"I can't," I argue. "I'll forget everything."

"Then I'll remind you when you wake up." His words sound like a threat, but he speaks them gently. "Go sleep," he repeats. "I need you sharp. I need you focused."

I can't disagree with him anymore. The truth is I'm too tired to have a clue what I'm doing.

I hate to feel like I'm giving up. I tell myself I won't really sleep. I'll just lie down here. Nice and cozy. Oh, a blanket. That's a surprising touch. I wouldn't think something like that would even enter Drisklay's head.

Do I need a pillow? he asks. No. I'm okay. I don't really plan to doze off. Just rest my eyes. I can use the quiet time to think. Think and try to remember.

The only thing I can't do is fall asleep. That's the promise I make to myself. That's the only reason I allow myself to roll to my side. Shut out the world. Curl up with my knees close to my chest. I'm tired, but I can stay awake a little while longer. This will just give me a chance to think.

There's got to be more memories stored in this dysfunctional brain of mine. Maybe if I'm real quiet and real still, they'll come to me.

I just have to stay awake. Whatever I do, I can't fall asleep …

CHAPTER 27

Springtime. I've always … No, wait. That's not right.

Where am I? Why did I fall asleep with the lights on?

"So, you're awake?"

I blink up at the man scowling at me then glance at the clock behind his shoulder. It's nine in the morning. How long have I been here? My back aches.

"Do you know who I am?" he asks, and his voice is uncharacteristically quiet. I'd say gentle, but that would be exaggerating. There's nothing soft about this man and there never has been in all the time I've known him.

I nod. "You're the detective."

I think I see him smile. At least, that's probably the closest he ever comes to smiling. "Good." He raises his Styrofoam cup as if toasting my memory.

I sit up. Something's missing. Something … my head. It doesn't hurt at all. What was in that coffee he gave me last night?

"Can you tell me what day it is?" Drisklay asks.

I think I know this one. "It's August," I answer.

His scowl is slightly less pronounced. "Do you know why you're here?"

"We were working on …" I glance at the table covered with Drisklay's crime scene photographs and remember. My stomach sinks. "Mom …"

"Right." He nods, looking pleased while I feel like I've just been punched in the gut.

"I remember …" I grope for words, staring at his desk for clues.

He leans in toward me intently. "Remember what?"

I don't know. I've just lost it. "I remember waking up," I tell him, feeling my way through my brain one word at a time. "I remember waking up and Dad telling me I was sick. And watching movies with my brother. And …" I squint at him, trying to get a better focus. "I remember you coming to our house. You've been there before."

Drisklay nods. "Sounds like your memories are coming back." It should be great news. I know it should be. But something still feels off. Some piece of the puzzle I still haven't connected yet.

"Can you tell me what happened when you went to your

cabin last May?" There's no hesitation. With Drisklay it's all about the investigation. No slowing down.

I try to think. What happened at the cabin?

I remember the crime scene photographs. I remember the details Drisklay told me. Mom was attacked in the house. Stabbed and bled to death. I was outside. Hit my head on the deck railing.

And Chris ... drowned. Is that what Drisklay said? Some fishermen pulled him out of the lake.

They're looking for the attacker. They're trying to find out who might have ...

My brain snaps alert as if it's been prodded with a Taser. I can feel my memory expanding with almost explosive speed.

"I remember," I tell him. "I know what happened."

A minute later, I'm in one of the questioning rooms. Drisklay has handed me a cup of lukewarm coffee and another Danish, but I'm not hungry or thirsty. I don't even need the caffeine to make sense of the memories swirling around in my brain.

I tell the detective everything.

CHAPTER 28

"Marco?" My voice is hurried. Desperate. I've locked myself in the bathroom of the cabin. A minute is all I have. All I have to save us both.

"Mia?" my brother asks. "Are you okay? I thought you were at the cabin."

I run the shower water for background noise and clutch my cell to my ear. "I am," I tell him, "but there's a problem. Chris is in trouble."

Marco doesn't say anything, and for a terrifying moment I'm afraid I've lost the connection.

"Marco?"

"I'm here." My brother's voice is flat. So emotionless it's almost eerie.

I want to tell him about the letter. Want to beg him to drive over to Chris's house and see if he can get into that truck before Mr. Gomez does. If we're lucky and if God answers my prayers, Chris's dad will never find out what his son wrote.

It's the only way I know to keep Chris safe.

"I have a favor to ask you," I begin. Something's wrong with Marco. I can tell by the way he's talking to me, or rather by the way he's not talking. But I can't worry about that now. There's no guessing what Mr. Gomez will do when he sees Chris's letter. I can't let that happen to him. Can't let that happen to us.

"Now's not a good time," Marco says. My palms are so sweaty I'm afraid I'll drop the phone and crack the screen.

"This is important," I tell him. "Chris is in trouble." When was the last time I asked Marco for anything? Doesn't he realize how serious this is? I wasn't joking when I told Chris his dad would kill him. I'm afraid for my boyfriend's safety.

Mine too, if I were to be totally honest.

I hear a loud commotion on the other end of the line. "Where are you?" I ask. It's too early for my brother to be at a bar or nightclub. What's he doing?

"Don't worry about me," Marco says. His voice is so low I have to strain to hear him. "Listen, there's something going on. Something I think you should know."

Yes, there's something going on. My boyfriend's in danger. If Mr. Gomez reads that note before Marco can get to it first …

"Is Chris with you?" Marco asks. His voice is so quiet he has to repeat the question a second time.

"He's outside," I answer, even though if I know Chris, he probably followed me into the cabin and is waiting right outside the bathroom door to talk to me. I turn the faucet to give the shower more water pressure, even though I'm not sure how well it covers up my side of the conversation. My brother and I are both whispering, both straining to hear each other speak.

"Mia, listen." Something about Marco's voice makes my heart catch in my throat. I feel dizzy and wonder if I still have a pulse. "Is Mom there?"

"What? No. She went to get some groceries. She'll probably be back in half an hour."

"That's not enough time. You and Chris need to get out of there now."

He's talking like a crazy man. Crazy and paranoid and doing everything except driving over to Chris's house to see if that letter is still in his dad's truck.

"We can't go anywhere. All our friends will be here soon."

"You aren't listening," Marco snaps, daring to raise his voice. "Chris is in danger."

It's the same thing I was trying to tell my brother all along, except I've got the horrible feeling we're not talking about the same danger at all.

"Mia?" There's a gentle knocking on the bathroom door.

It's Chris. "Mia, are you okay? Can you come out here and let me know you're okay?"

"What are you talking about?" I hiss into the phone.

"He'll probably kill me if I tell you this," Marco begins. I hate the fact that I don't have to ask him who he's talking about.

I sink to the bathroom floor, still hanging onto the phone with my sweaty hand and whisper to my brother, "I'm listening."

CHAPTER 29

"Are you feeling better now?" Chris asks when I step out of the bathroom. I stare out the window, as if the threat Marco warned me about is behind the cabin as we speak. The lake is calm, but my emotions are anything but.

"I'm sorry," he whispers. "I shouldn't have done anything without asking you first."

I don't know what to say. Can't even imagine where I'm supposed to begin. My brother's words are echoing in my ears. Words I'd never expect to believe. Except I do believe them.

"Is this about my dad?" Chris asks. "He really doesn't care what I do. And if he does, I'm graduating in a week. He can't dictate my life."

"What about your sister?" The longer we can keep this conversation focused on his family, the longer I have to compose my emotions. Get a hold of my thoughts. Decide how to escape. My eyes dart everywhere. I never noticed before just how many windows our cabin has.

"I've already called Gabrielle's grandma and told her everything. I can't explain it, Mia, but this is something I really need to do. I can't be afraid of him all my life. Gabrielle's grandma says she'll watch her. Or maybe I'll even move her in with me. I don't know. I just know that I have to do this. And I want you to be there with me."

It's this last part that makes me finally break down into tears. He doesn't understand. He doesn't understand anything.

It's my fault, really. He's told me everything about his family. Everything.

And he still knows nothing about mine.

"It isn't going to work," I tell him, burying my head against his chest. My body is trembling, but he feels strong against me.

Chris kisses the top of my head. I wish I could protect him from what I'm about to say.

I realize it would be infinitely easier if he broke up with me, and in that instant I know what I have to do. Know exactly what I have to say.

I pull away from him, not because I don't need his strength. I do. But I'm going to have to rely on my own determination and willpower now. I can't lean on him. Not anymore.

I make my way out the back door. Head toward the lake. He chases after me, just like I knew he would.

Halfway to the dock, I find my voice. "I can't marry you,

Chris. I'm sorry. It just won't work."

"I know." He's following me toward the water now, hasty in his attempts to reassure me. "That was impulsive. That was stupid. I have no idea why I even said those things earlier. Let's just forget it."

I keep my back to him so he can't see the tears streaking down my cheeks. I can't show him my face or he'll know. He'll know and then he'll try to protect me, try to make it right, and then we're both as good as dead.

The only thing I can do now is send him away, no matter how hard it hurts. No matter how much it kills me.

I take a deep breath. Ball my hands into fists. I think about what my brother just told me. I've got to do this.

"I can't marry you." I try to make my voice sound fierce, angry, but I'm not sure it works. I have to do a better job selling it. "I can't marry you," I repeat, more firmly this time.

He reaches out. Tries to grab me by the shoulder. I fling his hand away. "Don't touch me," I snap.

"Hey." He holds his hands up in innocence. "It's me. You know I would never hurt you."

He's forcing me to face him. Forcing me to look into his … No. I can't. I can't do this. Not when he's staring at me like that.

The water from the lake looms large and dangerous in my spinning field of vision. Mom was right. We're not safe here. What was I thinking? We should head toward the woods. Why did I lead us right to the lake? I spin around and stride toward the trees. Got to keep Chris behind me. Got to keep my eyes hidden or else he'll know.

"Hey." He's sprinting to keep up. Why does he have to be so devoted? "Mia, wait."

I stop but keep my body angled so he's staring at the back of my shoulder. I cross my arms. Tell myself I have to be strong. Remind myself that this is for him.

Everything I'm about to do, it's all for him.

"I don't want to talk to you," I stammer. It'll be easiest for him if I make him mad. If I act irrationally, if I provoke him right where it kills him the most, his love will turn to hate. Even someone as kind and good-hearted as Chris.

I hope.

"Are you mad at me for proposing?" he asks. "If you don't want to get married now, that's fine. We don't have to rush things. We don't have to ..."

"I'm not going to marry you ever," I bark, inhaling sharply to try to steady my nerves. I sense him taking a step back as if I've given him a physical blow, but I don't turn to look.

"Because of my dad?" His voice is pained. Close to its

147

breaking point. This isn't working.

"Yes, because of your dad." Once we're standing by our deck, I turn to face him. It's not hard pretending to be angry. In fact, I'm not pretending at all. The only difference is I'm not angry with him.

I just have to sell it. Got to be convincing.

Got to get him to storm off into those woods.

Please, God, I beg.

"Listen," Chris is pleading. "I already told you, he doesn't care what I do anymore. If you're worried that he's going to keep on giving us trouble ..."

"It's not that, Chris." I spit out his name like a curse. "It's not just your dad."

"Then what is it?"

"I don't want to be with you, okay? I've been doing a lot of thinking, and it's not going to work out. I'm going to New York in the fall. I'm going to become a doctor. I don't ... I can't ..."

I see the pain flash in his eyes as realization hits for the first time. "Is that what this is about?"

Sell it, Mia, I coax myself. "Think about it. You ever heard of a pastor married to an MD? What would people think? Listen. I'm going to school. I'm not wasting my life passing out bulletins at the back of a sanctuary and teaching Sunday school every single weekend. That's not the life I want."

I've got him. The pain in his expression is so intense I could reach my hand out and squeeze it. Now I've just got to push him over one more edge. Push him toward anger.

This is for him, I remind myself. *You have to do this if you want to protect him.*

If life was fair, I would be wearing Chris's ring right now. I'd tell him I didn't care about what his dad thought or said. Chris and I could move to New York together. Get married. Share an apartment. I could still go to school. We'd find money somewhere if he wanted to go to Bible college or wherever it is pastors get their training.

I can see Chris as a pastor. And I can see myself as a pastor's wife, notwithstanding the lies I've just told him.

I can see it. And the picture is beautiful.

But it's not a picture that's meant for us.

We're right on the edge. There's not going to be any recovery from this. The merciful thing now is to finish what I've started. Get it over and done with.

For his own good.

"I'm sorry," I tell him. "I didn't want to do this until after graduation, but we need to end things."

Chris's face is so pained I can hardly breathe. I know I'll remember that expression every single day of my life. I take one more step back, sidling up to the deck.

"I don't want to hurt you," is all I can get out, "but when all is said and done, it's really for the best."

Chris reaches out to grab my hand, but I yank it a way with a terse, "Just go away."

He takes another step closer.

"Don't touch me." I push him. Hard. He loses his balance. His hands reach forward, grabbing for me. I reach out, but momentum and gravity are my two worst enemies. I'm falling backward. My head hits something hard.

For a terrifying second, I don't see anything.

Next thing I know, Chris is kneeling down beside me. "Mia, are you okay? Hold on. Let me check your head. Don't move."

"Wait," I croak. There are tears on my cheeks, but it's impossible to tell if they're mine or his.

"Shh." He whispers. "We'll talk about us later. Right now, I just want to see if you're hurt. Don't worry. You're going to be fine. I just want to look and see …"

He puts his hand to the back of my head, and his expression changes from pain to surprise to fear. He pulls his fingers away from me, fingers covered in blood.

"This is my fault," he says. "Hold on. Let me get my phone. Should I call 911?"

"Just go," I whisper. I can't tell if I'm light-headed at the sight of so much blood or if it's a result of the injury itself. I know how bad this looks. "Just go," I prompt him. "You need to leave me. Someone's coming ..."

And then I pass out.

CHAPTER 30

I open my eyes to the sound of someone praying. "Please, God, let her be okay. Please, God, let her be okay."

I blink up at blinding sunlight boring holes through my eyes to the very back of my skull. The pain is more acute than any dentist drill. "Chris?"

"Thank God," he breathes. "I'm so sorry," he says. "I didn't mean for it to happen. This is all my fault. Are you still bleeding?"

He moves as if to touch the back of my head again, but I swat his hand away.

"Listen," I say, "we've got to get out of here." How long was I passed out for? "Give me your shirt," I demand.

"What?"

"Your shirt. Let me use it to slow down the bleeding." I've never been good seeing my own blood, but the adrenaline from my terror still hasn't left my system. I want nothing more than to pass out again and wake up completely pain free, but I know we've got to get moving if we're going to survive. I have no idea how much time we have left.

I try to sit up, but I'm too dizzy. The woods are out of the question now.

"Come on," I say. "There's a paddleboat in the shed. I'll need your help getting it out."

"Mia, what are you talking about? You're not going on the water like this."

"Please." I hold his gaze. Beg him to understand. "Please," I repeat, more softly this time. "We have to go."

"So you're not mad about your head?"

"Forget about my head." I use his shoulder to raise myself up. He puts his arm around me to keep me from falling.

"Mia," he protests, "you need to tell me what's going on."

"What's going on," I snap, "is we're both in serious danger. And now I need you to do exactly what I say."

I stumble toward the shed, Chris supporting the bulk of my weight. I'm dizzy, but I can't stop.

"We need to get the boat in the water," I tell him.

"Can't you tell me what's going on first?"

"Not until we're safe."

He looks at me once, then does what I say. We only find one life jacket, and Chris insists that I wear it. With the back of my head banged up so badly, I probably shouldn't argue.

Besides, there's no time.

No time at all.

Chris takes the oars. It's too difficult for me to sit on the platform, so I sink to the bottom of the boat and lean with my back against the siding. It's not the most comfortable position, not when I'm bundled up in the life jacket like this, but it's better than falling overboard.

"Mind telling me where we're going?" Chris asks.

"There's a trail I know on the far side over there. Once we get to land, I'll help you hide the boat."

"Mia ..."

"I know. I know." The sunlight is piercing through my skull. The pain in the back of my head has started to throb. But Chris needs answers.

He's going to hate me when he finds out, but I can't keep this from him. Not anymore.

Because I love him. Because I need to keep us both safe.

It's time to tell Chris the truth. All of it.

CHAPTER 31

"There's some things you don't know about my dad," I begin.

"Is this the part where you tell me he's in the mob? That once we get engaged, I'm in his circle of trust or whatever it's called?"

I'm not sure if he's joking or not. Right now, it doesn't matter. I hope Chris isn't planning to interrupt the whole time. It's going to be hard enough to explain what's going on when I'm so terrified. My head feels like my skull's broken in two.

"That's not it," I say. "Dad is … Well, you know my dad. He's got some pretty high-up connections."

Chris doesn't say anything. I'm thankful for the chance to move forward. To explain as best I can. I'm dizzy, except I don't know if that's because I hit my head or because I'm so terrified.

"He, um, well, he's involved in a lot of stuff …" I clear my throat. "And I've never told you this, but he has a pretty tragic backstory."

I wait for Chris to laugh and tell me it sounds like I'm talking about a supervillain or something, but he's focused on his rowing. I feel a little freer to talk as our family cabin gets smaller in the distance.

"I have a half-sister. *Had* a half-sister, I should say. From my dad's first marriage."

"Okay."

I take a deep breath. My head is throbbing, but I think the bleeding has slowed down at least. "When she was eighteen, she was found raped and murdered on a hiking trail."

"Geeze."

I choose to ignore Chris's one-word responses.

"So, um, we never really talked about her or anything, but I knew my dad never got over it. He tried really hard to figure out what happened. Hired private investigators and everything. The police eventually said it was a cold case, but Dad didn't give up. There was DNA evidence. It was ... Dad sent it to a private firm then had a friend run it against the police database." I swallow, having no idea how Chris is going to react to this next part. "It was your dad."

The rowing stops, but I don't look at Chris.

"My dad raped and murdered your sister?"

The sunlight reflects off the water, radiating agony through my retinas, aiming it directly to the back of my skull. I can't tell from Chris's expression what he's feeling. Incredulous? Disgusted? Defensive? Chris knows what his father's capable of, but having a monster of a father doesn't erase your sense of family loyalty.

Just look at me if you need a living example.

"They can't prove anything," I tell him. "If the police question your dad, he can claim their relationship was consensual and that he had nothing to do with the murder. But they aren't going to question him. My dad's friend made sure the DNA evidence they had at the station disappeared."

"Why? With all his connections, he could ..."

"I know," I interrupt. "But that's not the way my dad likes to deal with things."

Chris sets his jaw and doesn't respond. Now that I've gotten this much of the story out, it's the perfect time for him to interject. Anything. But he's silent.

We're getting close now to the bank. Wincing in pain, I point toward a spot with enough tree and shrub covering we can hide the boat. Hopefully, it will give us enough time to figure out what we're going to do next. We're just a few feet away from the shore when he says in a low voice, "You've known this about my dad the whole time we were together?"

157

"No. My brother just told me today, but he said Dad found out a couple months ago."

"So if he's known that long, why are we running away like this?"

I don't know what to say, and for a minute I'm afraid Chris might not believe anything I'm telling him. I'm not sure I can blame him, but I do have to make him understand. Make him realize how serious the situation really is.

"My dad's ... my dad's ..." I search for the right words. The right way to explain it. Chris may understand physical fear and terror, but he has no idea what it's like hiding the kind of secrets I have. My head has started to throb again, and I wonder if I'm still bleeding.

"There are other things he's done, too," I whisper, just loud enough for Chris to hear me over the sound of the oars. "He can be really dangerous."

"Then you should call the police. You should tell them ..."

"He's got people on the inside." There's no way Chris is going to understand. I've uncovered bits and pieces about Dad's illicit activities for years and still only know a fraction of what he's done.

Of what he's capable of.

"So now what?" Chris asks, pulling the boat up to the shore

and helping me out. I'm dizzy, the world swirling around me as I try to stand. "My dad killed your sister. Your dad's known about it for months. What does running to the other side of the lake fix?"

"You talked to my dad this morning, didn't you?" I need to put my thoughts together more coherently. Need to make Chris see what kind of danger we're in. He pulls the boat onto the shore, and I try to help him heft it behind some overgrown bushes.

"You talked to my dad," I repeat, leaning against a tree to support my unsteady weight. "And you told him you want to propose to me."

"Not that it was that successful of a proposal," Chris mumbles.

"That was for you," I tell him. "I was trying to get you to leave. Give me time to talk to my dad in private."

Chris gives me a scowl. "You're telling me that your father's in a murderous rage, and your plan was to just sit down and have a little heart to heart with him?"

I bristle at his tone. "He would never hurt me." I know I sound defensive, but I don't care. My dad might be involved in all kinds of activities he's worked hard to keep from the police and his family, but I know with absolute certainty that he would never raise a finger against me.

159

Not for anything.

Chris stands up. Sweat clings to his brow. "If your dad's going to come after my dad, then we need to go warn him. We shouldn't be out here hiding, especially not with your head bleeding like that."

And then I realize Chris still doesn't understand. "That's the thing," I tell him, ignoring the pain pulsing between my temples. "My dad isn't after your dad. Not that way. He wants him to suffer the same way he has."

Chris throws a few branches over the boat for a little extra cover and wipes his brow. "I have no idea what you're talking about."

"My dad knows what it's like to have his child brutally attacked and killed, right?"

"Right."

"Dad never got over what happened to his daughter," I say, trying hard to keep my voice steady, "And now he wants nothing more than for your dad to know the exact same kind of pain."

CHAPTER 32

I'm trying to find the strength to tell Detective Drisklay what happened once Chris and I started making our way down the trail when Sandy rushes in.

"There you are, sweetie. I got here as soon as I could. We had a late start today. Carl misplaced the keys, and Woong couldn't find his homework assignment, and ... Oh, listen to me babbling. I'm sorry. Mia, it's me, Sandy. From church?"

"I remember," I answer, returning her hug. "I remember everything."

She pulls back and looks at me closely. "Everything?"

I nod slowly.

"Oh, thank you, Jesus," Sandy sighs. "I had such a hard time sleeping last night, and I was just praying and praying and praying for you and asking God to heal your memory. I'm so glad to hear it." Sandy clasps her hands together and then gives me another hug. "Oh, it's a miracle. Officer Drisklay, I'm sorry to interrupt your work, but I've just got to tell the Lord how thankful I am." And right here, with the stoic detective looking on uncomfortably, Sandy prays for me.

"Sweet Savior Jesus," she breathes, "I bless you Lord for healing sweet Mia's mind. I bless you Lord for healing her memory and recovering what she lost. And now, Father, we lift up this investigation to you. We pray that whoever's responsible for the tragedy that impacted Mia and her family would be resolved in Jesus' name. We pray for justice, Lord. Justice as well as redemption because we know there isn't a single soul on earth worthy of your love or your grace or your forgiveness. And so I ask, sweet and merciful Savior, that whoever hurt Mia and her family would be punished appropriately according to the law but also find forgiveness and grace through the blood that Jesus Christ shed on his cross to take the punishment for our sins."

I sense Drisklay shifting uncomfortably and wonder if Sandy's prayer is about to turn into an altar call. Finally, she wraps it up and gives me one last hug. "I didn't know if you'd had anything to eat besides Officer Drisklay's old Danishes, so I baked you some muffins. I've got blueberry and chocolate here. Now I have to warn you, they're not too sweet because of Carl and his health. I have to cook different now, you know. Baking's a whole new ball game when you have a diabetic in the house. There's no sugar in here, just a little bit of honey. I'm still not all that fond of whole grain flour either, but it's so much better for you. At least that's what they say. So here you are." She sets an overflowing paper bag on the table in front of me and invites Drisklay to help himself as well.

"I'm fine," he says, holding up his Styrofoam cup of coffee like a soldier's salute.

"I can't stay long," Sandy says. "I just hated the thought of you waking up here all alone and scared without any of your memories." Sandy pauses and tilts her head to the side, staring at me as if she's trying to decide something. Finally, she leans forward and kisses me on the cheek. "Well, darling, I'm just so glad you're doing better. It's a gift, I tell you. A true gift. And a miracle too. A real answer to prayer."

Drisklay clears his throat, and Sandy clasps her hands together. "Well, I'll leave you two to your investigating, but call me if you need anything. Anything at all. Shall I stop back by around lunchtime?"

Drisklay eyes the paper bag. "I think we'll keep from getting too hungry."

"Just remember, a growing girl needs more than cold coffee and danishes," Sandy wags her finger at Drisklay before bustling out the door.

I haven't touched the food in the bag yet even though the

thought of muffins is deliciously tantalizing.

"She's got a good point," I tell Drisklay.

"Who? The pastor's wife?"

"Yeah. I'm not sure I've been this clear-headed since the accident. And I don't think it's because that chair is the most comfortable bed I've slept in. Think it's just a coincidence?"

I'm glad Sandy isn't here. She'd probably think my question was blasphemy. I have no doubt that God could have restored my memory in some miraculous way last night. But if he wanted to do that, couldn't he have done it months earlier, when the information I have could have helped the investigation along that much faster?

"I have a few theories of my own on that," Drisklay says dryly. "That's why I've ordered a blood test."

"Blood test?"

He lets out a sigh. "May as well tell you now. When we were searching your home, we found the pills your father was giving you. Your pain medicine. Apparently, you were on very heavy doses of a new drug currently being tested for the treatment of anxiety. One of the most common side-effects, however, especially at the dose I believe you were given, is short-term memory impairment."

"Wait a minute." I try to remember. Pain pills? Short-term

memory impairment? "My dad was drugging me?"

Drisklay sighs. "I wish it were as simple as that."

"What do you mean?"

He leans forward. "Miss Blanca, I'm going to need to ask you some uncomfortable questions about your family. Starting with your brother Marco."

I blink. My brother? But why? How is he involved in any of this?

"Marco?" is all I can think to say.

Drisklay nods. "I understand he's in pharmaceutical sales." Oh. That's what this is about. They think that since Marco might have had access to new and experimental drugs, he's somehow implicated.

"I don't think he'd get involved in anything like this," I say. "He wouldn't be working for my dad. They don't even like each other. And he's the one who warned me and Chris, remember?"

Drisklay passes me an envelope. "Do you know what this is?"

I stare at the file with my brother's name printed on the tab then shake my head.

"Over the past several years, five different women have come forward with accusations against your brother, all of them quite serious. I can assure you that the evidence against him is more than circumstantial, so do you care to guess why this file

165

is so thin?"

"I don't know," I answer, even though a gnawing suspicion has settled into the base of my skull.

"Apparently, your father has quite the list of connections. None of these alleged victims carried through with their reports, and some of the incriminating evidence mysteriously disappeared from our labs as well. Do you get what I'm saying?"

"I think so," I admit.

"I'm saying that even if your father and your brother weren't lovey-dovey, all your dad had to do was wave this file over your brother's head. That feels like pretty good incentive to cooperate with Daddy, don't you think?"

I don't answer. I want to go back to sleep, wake up, and imagine it's senior skip day all over again.

"Marco was there to help me." My protest is as weak as my body feels. "He was ... we watched movies together," I conclude lamely.

Drisklay doesn't acknowledge my non sequitur, sparing me further indignity.

"So here's what I think happened," he says. "Daddy found out who it was that killed his daughter all those years ago. Or at least he had his suspicions, and he was willing to circumvent the law to act on them."

I don't reply. Suddenly, Sandy's muffins no longer sound so appealing.

"Daddy wanted to get revenge through the son," Drisklay continues, "but he knew you were dating him, so he decided to wait it out. For all I know, he didn't want to upset you and was waiting for the two of you to break up before he made his move. Just because someone's a monster of a human being doesn't make them a terrible parent."

I pause, realizing that in a single sentence, Drisklay has explained a paradox that's plagued me for years.

"But you and Lover Boy didn't break up," he goes on, "and one Friday last May, Daddy got a call from your boyfriend talking about marriage. That's when he discovered how serious a relationship you two were in. He'd never give you away to the son of the man who raped and killed his daughter. So that's our motive right there. Daddy comes out to the cabin. Makes his move. Next thing you know, two people are dead, your boyfriend and your mother. I'm going to give your father the benefit of the doubt and guess he didn't mean to kill his wife. Maybe she was trying to stop him. Trying to protect you and he got mad when she stood in his way. That's for the crime scene techs to figure out, not me.

"Now, Daddy's got two victims, one intentional, one not.

167

He dumps Gomez's body in the lake, trusting the mud and silt to do their work to hide the corpse. As for you, now he's only got two choices. He can kill so you can't ever testify against him, or he can mess with your memories. He doesn't want to hurt you, plus he's got access to the right kind of drugs, thanks to your brother and his job."

My head is swirling, and I'm trying desperately to keep up.

"How is that sounding so far?" Drisklay asks.

I want to argue. I want to defend my family.

But I have nothing to say.

"So we've got our motive and our means down," Drisklay concludes. "Now all I need you to do is tell me the rest of the story. Tell me exactly what happened when you and Gomez got to the other side of the lake."

CHAPTER 33

After we've traveled about half a mile down the trail, Chris insists we stop. With my head injury, I'm in no shape to keep hiking. I need a break.

He wraps his arms around me. I feel tired. So tired. "Are you hanging in there?" he says. "Don't go to sleep on me, all right? You've got to stay awake."

"I'll try," I promise him.

He smiles down at me. "Tell me something."

"What?"

"Did you really mean it when you said you never wanted to marry me?"

I want to laugh. I want to cry. I want to feel his lips pressed against mine.

But even more than that, I want to sleep.

"I didn't mean it," I answer.

Chris grins again. "I didn't think so."

"I was scared for you," I admitted. "I thought that ..."

169

Chris shushes me. "I get it. You don't need to explain."

Surrounded by trees and bushes, we're staying to the side of the trail so we can stay more easily hidden. At least I hope we're hidden. I'm staring up at the bright blue sky, at the leaves rustling gently in the breeze. A pair of birds passes by overhead.

"Don't fall asleep." Chris gives me a little shake.

"Huh, what?"

"Don't fall asleep," he repeats.

"I wasn't."

"What are we going to do now?" he asks after a minute.

I need to think, but my head hurts too much. Why am I always the one who has to come up with the plan?

"Run away with me," Chris says.

"What?"

"I'll take you someplace far from here. Someplace where your dad will never find us. We'll be safe. We'll be together. We'll be ..."

I press my finger against his mouth. Was that the wind? I'm certain I heard something.

Chris leans forward and whispers in my ear. "I'm serious, Mia. I know you didn't mean what you said back there. I know you thought that the only way to keep me safe was to break up with me. But think about it. Even if we break up, that's not going to stop your dad if he wants to come after me, right? So either we go to the police, or we ..."

"No police," I interrupt. Wasn't he listening to anything I said? Doesn't he realize my dad has contacts everywhere?

"Okay. Okay. No police. I just thought that ..." Chris sighs. "So there's only one option. You run away with me. We'll find someplace. I've got a cousin in Missouri. We can pool our money together. Take a train ..."

I shake my head, even though each time I move, my brain feels like someone's swinging a baseball bat against my skull. "Don't you think he can figure out about your cousin in Missouri?"

"We'll find somewhere else then," Chris insists. "We'll run to Canada. Mexico. Come on. There's gotta be someplace."

He's right. He's right about everything. Breaking up won't solve our problems. Our only hope is if we stay together.

"I just want to keep you safe." He's holding me close, and my blood is smeared across his forearm. He still has his shirt off, but he feels just as warm and just as protective as if we were wrapped in a king-sized duvet.

"Come on," he says. "We should start by getting you to a hospital. You need stitches or something for your head. Then we'll figure out how much money we have, see where we can go ..."

I squeeze my eyes shut. How can he make it sound so easy? How can we just leave everything behind? Our graduation. Our friends.

My mom …

"I don't feel so good," I say.

Chris takes a look at my head. He must think I'm talking about my injury. He scoops me up in his arms. "It's going to be okay," he assures me. "When I had that dream, when God showed me that I'm going to become a pastor and make you my wife, I made him a promise. I promised him I'd take care of you no matter what. Give you the shirt off my back." He chuckles and looks down at his bare arms. "Guess he took me literally."

I want to laugh when he says this. I really do. Want to believe this is all going to work out. That Chris and I can just walk out of these woods, bandage my bleeding head, and make our escape. Canada? Mexico? Why not? Other people have run away before. Disappeared.

Am I ready to leave everything else behind? Everything but Chris?

And does it really matter? Now that Chris knows, now that I've told him everything, neither of us are safe here. We have to get out. We have to …

Chris stops in the trail. "Did you hear that?" he whispers, crouching us both down behind a tree trunk. I'm still in his arms, my biceps tense and sore from clinging to him so tightly.

"It's going to be okay," he whispers into my ear. "I'm going to keep you safe. I promise."

"Mia! Mia!" It's my dad. He's found us already. How did he get here so fast? How did he know we were on the other side of the lake?

"Stay here," Chris tells me. "I'll take care of this."

"Mia!" Dad shouts. He's not near us yet. If Chris got a running start …

"You go," I hiss in Chris's ear.

"What? You're crazy."

"Go," I tell him, pleading. "You can run faster than he can. Go. I'll stay here. Distract him when he comes by."

Chris is looking at me like I've grown purple eyebrows. "I'm not leaving you here all by yourself."

"I'll be all right," I assure him. My dad is a very dangerous man, but he would never hurt me.

Never.

And in an instant, I know. This is what I can do. This is how I can save the man I love.

Back by the dock, I was ready to make Chris believe I'd stopped loving him. I was ready to make him think I hated him if that's what it took to save his life.

In the end, I think I knew it had to end this way. I give him what I know will be our last kiss.

"Go," I tell him. "Don't tell me where you're going. Don't write to me when you get there. Just be safe and start your life over."

"I won't leave you here." His voice is stubborn, and each second he hesitates my father is getting closer. Pretty soon, I won't be able to protect Chris at all.

"Please," I beg. "Do this for me."

I press my forehead against his. Assure him once more that I'll be safe. "My dad will never lay a finger on me," I promise.

"I'll never stop loving you," Chris whispers, holding me close for one last second. "Remember that," he says, his eyes steady. "Don't ever forget."

I'm not sure if it's his words or something in his gaze that tells me what he's planning. Or maybe I just know him so well.

"No, don't!" I shout. It doesn't matter now if Dad hears where we are or not. I try to grab Chris's hand, but he's already darting down the trail.

Back toward the lake.

Straight toward my father.

CHAPTER 34

Detective Drisklay scowls and waves away the junior detective who props the door open to see if we want more coffee.

"And that's the last thing you remember?" Drisklay asks me with a frown.

"That's the last thing I remember," I repeat.

Drisklay sighs. "Well, I imagine it's not quite rocket science to figure out what happened next. Gomez played the hero, got his body dumped in the lake, and Daddy took you home along with a whole arsenal of drugs to make you forget."

My whole body started trembling at some point when I began talking about hiding in the woods with Chris, and it hasn't stopped since. "What about Mom?" My voice is barely louder than a croak.

"We still don't know if your dad attacked her before or after he killed Gomez. To be honest, I'm not sure the timeline really matters."

"Why couldn't you figure this all out before?" I don't mean to sound accusatory, but it doesn't make sense to me. "Don't you always look at the family first?"

"Your father had an alibi," Drisklay says. "We have records of him chartering a flight on his business jet to Florida that morning as well as footage of him at his offices in Miami."

"So that was all doctored?"

Drisklay shrugs. "That's for the prosecution to determine."

I don't say anything else. It certainly makes sense. If Dad could wave his hand to make the allegations against my brother disappear, if he could kill his own wife as well as my boyfriend, he certainly would have found ways to cover his tracks.

"What happens now?" I ask.

Drisklay leans back in his chair and takes another sip of coffee.

"Now we do what we can to put your father behind bars and make sure he never gets out."

"Is that going to work?" I ask. "Is there enough evidence?"

"I've sent off your blood work to the lab already. If they find what I'm certain they're going to find, that's a good start."

"But what if he just blames my brother?"

"I'm sure he will," Drisklay continues. "Which is why I have men bringing Marco in right now. This file right here."

Drisklay taps on the envelope with my brother's name on it. "I think your brother's going to have some compelling reasons to cooperate with us."

I stare at the table. Think about what lies ahead. I shake my head. "You don't know my dad," I tell Drisklay. "You don't know how good he is at getting out of stuff like this."

Drisklay leans forward. "Miss Blanca, I didn't become the head detective here because I treat justice like a game. I'm here because I put men slimier, sleazier, and even more well-connected than your father behind bars for a living. And that's exactly what I intend to do here. Now." He stands up. "If you'll excuse me for a minute, I've got a pile of evidence in my favor and one sick and twisted son of a gun to get off the streets."

CHAPTER 35

Early fall. A crisp, breezy morning. I hear the rustling leaves outside the window of Sandy's guest room.

It's comfortable here. I've probably slept better in the past six weeks than I have since the incident last spring. Of course, getting myself off those drugs my dad and brother were slipping me has helped tremendously.

I suppose in a way Sandy was right. Even though there's a medical explanation for my memory's return, the fact that I'm here at all, that I'm safe, is nothing short of a miracle.

Marco got called into the police station the same day my memories came back. It didn't take Drisklay long to convince him to testify. Which means they're going after Dad next. I try to remember what Drisklay told me that day in his office. Just because someone's a monster doesn't make them a bad parent.

I wonder if it's normal to feel sorry for my dad. And guilty since I'm the reason he's in so much trouble.

Sandy's been amazing, of course. Said I can stay here as

178

long as I need. I can think clearly now and form new memories, but I never did recover everything I lost last summer. It's probably just as well. I can't imagine the trauma of having to learn each and every day Mom and Chris are dead.

It's even worse knowing that my Dad's to blame.

Let's just say I'm glad that chapter in my life is coming to an end.

Sandy has something she wants me to watch when I'm ready. Someone made a video of Chris's funeral last summer. I couldn't go. I was entrenched in police interviews, and for the first few weeks coming off the drugs, my senses were easily overwhelmed by crowds and loud noises. I heard the service was pretty amazing. Something like a hundred people came forward and asked for prayer. Most of them were teens from school or the youth group. A big chunk of them have become Christians.

So maybe Chris's dream of becoming a preacher and telling so many people about Jesus came true after all.

Right now, my life consists of morning devotions with Sandy and her family, lots of naps, and meetings with Drisklay. I guess that's going to be the story of my life for the next several months. Meetings and lawyers and appointments all the time. I've had a couple different doctors give me full exams to make sure my brain's recovered. That and to ensure I'm healthy enough to testify at my father's trial.

I did a Google search of that drug Marco stole from his company, the one Dad kept slipping me to make me unable to remember. Apparently it's been used with PTSD victims to make them forget their trauma entirely. I'm not sure how I feel about that. I'm just glad to have my normal brain back. It's kind of creepy when you sit down and think about how much one little pill can impact everything. Make you lose your memory. Your entire identity, really.

Like I said, I'm glad I don't remember those three months last summer.

I missed graduation, but I was awarded my diploma anyway. Sandy drove me by my old school a few weeks ago to pick it up. She's called NYU on my behalf too, and they've agreed to defer my scholarship. Some people take a gap year to travel the States or backpack across Europe. Looks like I'm taking a gap year to testify against my own father.

My emotions have evened out as my body finally purged the drugs from my system. I'm still devastated. Still miss my mom more than words can express. And I know I'll remember that determined look on Chris's face for the rest of my life. Both he and my mom died protecting me. I guess that's supposed to make me feel thankful. Maybe gratitude will come later. At this moment, I just feel guilty. Sandy has a friend who's a grief counselor. Says she's ready to talk with me whenever I feel strong enough to come in. There's no rush. My job is to get by day to day. It's still disorienting to wake up and recall that my mom and boyfriend are dead and my father's the one responsible.

Some days I wish I could forget again. Just for a little while.

I know I have a lot to be thankful for. I've been reading my Bible a lot when Sandy's out running errands or busy getting dinner ready. I still don't know why God allowed so many terrible things to happen to me and the people I love most, but I guess he's never promised to give us all the answers. He's just promised to walk beside us in our sorrows.

I've found the Psalms especially comforting these past few weeks.

It's early, but I hear Sandy puttering around in the kitchen. I'm surprised she doesn't wake up the entire cul de sac when she's in there cooking. Pretty soon, I'll get dressed. Head down the hall. See if Sandy needs a hand setting the table or pulling her whole wheat muffins out of the oven.

There's a Bible verse I read the other day. It's another one from Psalms. *God sets the lonely in families, he leads out the prisoners with singing.*

It's hard to describe how disorienting it is to lose your entire family in a day. To find out that your mom has been killed and your brother and father are both implicated. It's even weirder trying to describe what I feel when I think about losing Chris. Sometimes I'm not sure if I should say my boyfriend is dead or my fiancé is dead. It feels to me like neither word describes who he was or what he meant to me.

Some days I wake up furious at him. He should have never taken off down that trail. I could have stalled my dad. There's no way he would have hurt me. It could have given Chris the chance to get away. I'm mad at him for playing the hero, mad at him for dying. Mad at him for leaving me so alone. And then I remember that verse from Psalms.

God sets the lonely in families ...

In a few minutes, I'll join hands around a table with Sandy and her son as her husband thanks God for the food. While we eat breakfast, Sandy will pray over the names on her various lists and her husband will read a passage from the Bible and out of that morning devotion book he loves. It will never replace what I've lost. Never make me forget the pain I've suffered.

But maybe the point isn't to forget.

Maybe the point is to keep on remembering.

CHAPTER 36

Springtime. I've always loved the spring. And today's going to be perfect. Time to get myself up and out of bed.

Ow.

That sun sure is bright in my eyes. I love that Sandy has let me take over her guest room all these months. I just wish she had slightly better blinds. What this room needs are some heavy-duty blackout curtains.

A knock from the hallway. "Mia." Sandy's voice is cheerful. Melodic. Sometimes I miss Mom's *rat-a-tat-tat* on my door so much it hurts.

"I'm awake," I tell her.

The door slowly opens, and Sandy's standing there in her flowered skirt, her hair hanging in one long French braid. Wispy strands of gray stick out around her temples. I hope I'm as beautiful as she is when I reach her age.

She gives me a smile. "You still want to do this?" she asks. "The weather's holding out nicely. I think it's going to be a beautiful day."

I nod my head.

I'm ready.

Strange to think it's taken this long for me to get to this point. The grief counselor I've been seeing says that I probably needed to get through all the pre-trial hearings first. Once I sorted out some of my fear and other emotions wrapped around my dad, I could walk through all the other steps of grief.

And there have been many.

It's strange losing two people at once. Some weeks I cry myself to sleep every night because I'll never walk down the aisle and marry Chris. Other times, something will remind me of Mom, and I'll wonder how I could ever think that my fiancé's death could cause half the same level of despair that comes from losing a parent.

My counselor's right. There's been a lot of fear. Once I started talking to Drisklay and everyone else involved in the case, I realized there were even more things about my dad, secrets of his I'd been hiding for years. My testimony alone would be enough to land him with a dozen life sentences. Thankfully, my brother's agreed to testify as well, even though Marco's still in jail for crimes of his own.

Today marks the one-year anniversary of the day that

changed all our lives. The day that was wiped out of my memory for so long. After breakfast, Sandy and I are going over to Chris's grave. A few of my old friends from high school will be there. Kelsie's coming back from New York to meet us at the cemetery. A few others will be there too.

I feel a little guilty that it's taken me this long before I've felt ready to watch the recording of Chris's funeral. Like maybe that means I loved him less than I thought I did. Sandy tells me to be patient with myself, that everyone heals at different rates.

I'm glad I'm finally ready today.

At breakfast, the devotion we read is from Charles Spurgeon, one of Carl's favorite preachers.

Our spirit, attracted by the tempting glare, darts into the halls of pleasure, but soon is frightened and alarmed by the rough voice of conscience and the demands of insatiable passions.

It's taken me a while to understand the style of language Spurgeon writes in, but Carl reads him often enough I'm getting into the flow of it.

Man, without God, is like the mariner in the story, condemned to sail on forever, and never to find a haven.

I think back to my lost months, forever gone from my memory. If God hadn't intervened, would my imprisonment have endured indefinitely?

Long have you tugged the oar of ambition, or of the lust of pleasure, or of avarice, or of care. But rest a moment, I pray you, and listen to the witness of those who declare to you that escape from bondage is possible, and that rest is to be found even now.

I glance over at Sandy, who's beaming lovingly at her husband. Sometimes it hurts to watch how close Carl and Sandy are, to realize that I'll never share that kind of relationship with Chris. Other times it's comforting to know that happiness still exists in this world.

What if your chains should be broken today, and your labors should be ended, and you should enter into perfect peace! If so, it will be the gladdest Sabbath that your soul ever knew.

Carl pauses to explain that Spurgeon is speaking of heaven here. Early on, in those first few weeks of meetings and hearings and mourning, people would tell me I should be glad because my mom and Chris are both in a better place. I hated hearing that then. If heaven's so great, why couldn't God have let me die and join them there as well?

But I'm starting to understand a little more. I even have a letter I'm going to leave at Chris's gravesite today. I did the same thing for Mom several months ago, but I didn't feel ready for Chris's until now.

And others shall share in the gladness, for we who may be privileged to help you shall participate in your joy, and even spirits before the throne of God shall rejoice when they hear that another weary one has found rest in Christ Jesus.

I definitely know the weariness that Spurgeon's talking about. I know what it is to be so depressed you don't have the energy to leave your bed. I know what it's like to have mental fog so heavy it's exhausting just to get out a string of two or three sentences.

But I know that peace he's talking about too. Not the peace I'll experience in heaven. That day's probably still decades off in my case. But I've felt the hint of it, the echo of heavenly music. The promise of divine healing.

I think about the verse Carl and Sandy's son read just a few minutes earlier at family devotions where Paul's talking to the Philippian church. *I know what it is to be in need, and I know what it is to have plenty. I have learned the secret of being content in any and every situation.*

In spite of everything that's happened, I know God is with me, and I know he's used the things I've gone through in this past year to shape me into the woman I am. In just a few more months I'll be enrolling at NYU with a major in biology and minor in Spanish. I still want to become a doctor. I still want to open free healthcare clinics along the border. I feel like God's given me a second chance at life, and I definitely don't want to waste it.

After breakfast, I help Sandy clear the table. While she's cleaning up the dishes, I retreat to the quiet of her guest room. I pull out my phone and find the YouTube video where Chris's funeral's been recorded. Strange to think that a year ago today, I was eating breakfast with my mom and boyfriend. I wonder if Chris was thinking about that dream of his, the one where he was standing in front of a church preaching about Jesus.

I read the description on the YouTube video. *Celebration of life service for Chris Gomez, who went to be with the Lord on May 24, three weeks before he turned 19.*

There's no mention of his murder. That's all. *Celebration of life service.*

I could stay in Sandy's guest room all morning staring at the thumbnail, reading the description, trying to guess what life would have been like if Chris hadn't been killed.

Or I could sit down, press play, and finally say goodbye to the man I loved.

I know exactly what choice I'm going to make.

CHAPTER 37

"Chris Gomez was a student, athlete, and friend." Pastor Carl's voice is as rich and booming as always. After a short introduction, the worship band gets on stage. I don't think I can handle the emotional dam that will break if I listen to the music, so I skip ahead. I can always come back to the singing part later.

"Before God called him home," Carl says a little later, "Chris lived his life for the Lord. He served here in the church. He volunteered with our local outreaches and was active in the youth group. Based on what I've heard from his fellow students, there wasn't a single soul Chris wasn't willing to help. But that's not why I'm convinced his spirit is in heaven today. Plenty of good people live good lives and do good things, but if you die without knowing the grace and forgiveness of Jesus Christ, the Bible says you're still lost in your sins.

"But Chris knew the grace of Jesus. In fact, I had the immense blessing and honor of sitting with him one night after youth group and praying with him while he asked God to forgive his sins. It was at that moment Chris's soul was saved for eternity, and a few weeks later I had the privilege and honor to baptize him right here in this church.

"Chris will always be remembered as a kind spirit. A gentle and compassionate soul who loved God and loved others and thus fulfilled the two greatest commandments in all of Scripture. The morning before he died, Chris wrote this in his journal, and it's with his family's permission I'm sharing it with you here today.

"*Last night,* Chris writes, *I had a dream. I was standing in front of a church, telling everyone there about Jesus. I didn't feel stage fright. I didn't feel nervous at all. I think it means God wants me to become a pastor. I feel scared and honored that he chose me for a calling like this.*"

Carl looks up from the piece of paper he's holding and smiles at his congregation. "Friends," he concludes, "One of the saddest aspects of performing a funeral for someone this young is that Chris died with plans unfulfilled. With dreams unattained. You heard it in his own words. Chris had received a calling to go into the ministry, a calling I have no doubt he would have followed and obeyed if he'd remained alive. And not only that, he would have excelled in it. Why? Because like I said before, Chris loved God and Chris loved people. There's no better recipe for a pastor.

"Chris never had the chance to go to seminary. Never finished a Bible college degree or got ordained. He never held office in a church. Never officiated at a wedding or a funeral.

"But that doesn't mean Chris didn't fulfill his calling. Today there are hundreds of people gathered here. Many of you are young. Many of you are Chris's friends from school. Some of you have never set foot in a church building before. Some of you have never heard the good news that Jesus died to forgive your sins and purchased your way to heaven with his own blood.

"Chris isn't standing before you today preaching. He isn't holding up his Bible, urging you to be saved, encouraging you in the Lord. But I'm here to tell you that Chris has fulfilled his calling once and for all, because a godly life and testimony is the greatest sermon anyone on this planet can ever preach. And Chris lived his life and testimony with honor, with grace, and with love. And if he were here today, if he were standing here behind this pulpit, looking at you seated here in this sanctuary right now, he would urge each and every one of you who doesn't know Christ as your personal Lord and Savior to accept God's love for you. To ask God to forgive you for your sins. To acknowledge that Jesus is the one and only way to heaven, to submit your lives in obedience to his Word and to enjoy the riches of blessings that come from belonging to the family of God.

"If you'd like to make that decision right now," Carl says, "I'd like to ask you to step forward."

Sandy's told me before about this part of the service. She's mentioned the number of Chris's and my friends who walked down that aisle. But still, I'm surprised to see how quickly the crowd gets to their feet. How they're practically racing one another to the front where volunteers are standing by to pray with each and every one of them.

I miss Chris with all of my heart. I thought it might get easier with time, but so far it hasn't. Still, everything Carl said at the funeral is true. Chris did live out his calling. He did preach the gospel, even without knowing it.

Now he's gone. He can't preach anymore, although I suppose people like me can still be blessed and encouraged by watching his funeral. I think about what Carl said, that a godly life and testimony is the most powerful sermon you could ever preach. If I can remind myself of that each and every day I'm on this earth, I have the feeling I'll be helping Chris share the gospel with others too, just like we were doing together in his dream.

I need to remember when life gets hard to look past my own

circumstances. To see past my own fears and pain. To remember that no matter how bleak life gets, God is good, and God is with me.

And that's a lesson I pray I'll never forget.

Made in the
USA
Monee, IL